SHORT STORY SSi INTERNATIONAL

**Tales by the World's
Great Contemporary Writers
Presented Unabridged**

D1304591

All selections in
Short Story International
are published full and
unabridged.

Editor
Sylvia Tankel

Associate Editor
Erik Sandberg-Diment

Contributing Editor
John Harr

Assistant Editors
Mildred Butterworth
Debbie Kaufman
Kirsten Hammerle

Art Director
Charles J. Berger

Circulation Director
Nat Raboy

Production Director
Michael Jeffries

Business Manager
John O'Connor

Publisher
Sam Tankel

Volume 15, Number 86, June 1991.
Short Story International (USPS 375-970)
Copyright © by International Cultural
Exchange 1991. Printed in U.S.A. All rights
reserved. Reproduction in whole or in part
prohibited. Second-class postage paid at
Great Neck, N.Y. 11022 and at additional
mailing offices. **Editorial offices: P.O. Box
405, Great Neck, N.Y. 11022.** Enclose
stamped, self-addressed envelope with
submission. One year (six issues) subscription
for U.S., U.S. possessions $24, Canada $27
(US), other countries $29 (US). Single copy
price $5.45 (US). **For subscriptions and
address changes write to *Short Story
International*, P.O. Box 405, Great
Neck, N.Y. 11022.** *Short Story
International* is published bimonthly by
International Cultural Exchange, 6 Sheffield
Road, Great Neck, N.Y. 11021. Postmaster
please send Form 3579 to P.O. Box 405,
Great Neck, N.Y. 11022.

Note from the Editor

Why is it that thorns creep into the relationships of people, no matter what culture or country you consider?

In this issue, "A Wedding in Zhaojiatun" presents a poor and honest Chinese official who goes out of his way to attend his cousin's son's wedding. There the official's cousin, whom he loves and who was his lifeline when he was a youngster, turns from him because he will not hand in a dishonest report to enrich the cousin.

In "Unspoken Words" a dying father in Argentina is visited by his son. The old man can no longer speak but his thoughts bespeak his happiness in seeing his son whom he has yearned to see through the many years the son was too busy making a name for himself to make time for his father. In "Hunger" a young Egyptian learns of his wealthy father's neglect of his injured workers when he stops a former employee from committing suicide.

"Fish Soup," set in Zambia, demonstrates how childish and petulant adults can be. And "Thou Shalt Not Make..." takes us into the life of a famous Russian journalist who, since he was fifteen, has carried the image of an Italian movie star in his heart and let it influence his relationship with his wife, his son, his whole life.

"Accident" tells of Uganda, Idi Amin's Uganda, and how a white woman learns why she was humiliated. The color of one's skin is also significant in "A Point of Identity" which defines "black," "colored" and "white" in South Africa.

Scotland's Roderick Wilkinson's "Crunch Point" takes place in the USA where, with humor and wisdom, an older man staves off a younger man bent on wrecking his marriage.

These stories, along with the other meaningful stories in this issue, provide deep insights into the similarities and differences in human relationships throughout our ever-changing and still imperfect world.

Copyrights
and acknowledgments

We wish to express deep thanks to the authors, publishers, translators and literary agents for their permission to publish the stories in this issue.

"Unspoken Words" by Daniel Moyano, translated by H.E. Francis, appeared in *Partisan Review*, 1988. Copyright © 1968 Daniel Moyano. "Within Four Walls" by Stephen Kelen appeared in the *London Courier*. Copyright Stephen Kelen. "A Flying Visit" by Eric Cameron originally appeared in *The Atlantic Advocate*. Copyright 1989 Eric Cameron. "A Wedding in Zhaojiatun" by Ma Qide appeared in *Chinese Literature*, 1988. Translation by Wen Xue. By permission. "Hunger" from *A Selection of Short Stories* by Naguib Mahfouz. Prism *v*. Published by the Ministry of Culture and Information, Egypt. By permission. "First Prize to Miss Pettigrew" by Carey Blyton. Copyright © Carey Blyton. "Summer of the Amphora" by Francis Ebejer, 1991. "Tuatara" by Cecilia Dabrowska originally appeared in *Blackwood's*. Copyright Cecilia Dabrowska. "Crunch Point" by Roderick Wilkinson. Copyright Roderick Wilkinson. "A Point of Identity" from *Renewal Time* by Es'kia Mphahlele. Published by Readers International. Copyright © Readers International. "Accident" by Lino Leitão originally appeared in *The Massachusetts Review*. Copyright Lino Leitão. "Fish Soup" by Richard Armstrong originally appeared in the *Amherst Review*. Copyright Richard Armstrong. "Thou Shalt Not Make..." by Victoria Tokareva appeared in *Soviet Literature*, 1989. Translation by Vladimir Korothky. By permission.

Table of Contents

"When I was a young father and you an indifferent son, your coldness made me despair."

Unspoken Words

BY DANIEL MOYANO

MY son, I knew that I would see you once more before I die. Doña Dora, when she talks to me, often says my son is an ungrateful thing and I'll never see him again. Your visit, which can be nothing but a show of affection, is proving how wrong she was.

I'm a little ashamed that you find me in this condition, which I'm now used to. For me the degradation until getting to this stage has been very slow, and my situation doesn't surprise me now when, by coming here, you set me once more back into the world of desires. Besides, I'm the actor in this situation. But for you, who played no part in the small events which put me in this place, my illness is a sudden thing; and since, besides, you are the spectator, no doubt I'm now a terrible thing for you to see.

I look at you and it seems a lie to have you so near. I haven't seen you for many years. You've kissed me and now you talk to me about so many things, carefully choosing, as everyone does, words which require no answers. So I know beforehand everything you can say to me. You even use the same tone of voice which everyone uses with me, as if it were a suitable tone to contact my memory directly. You speak to me and meanwhile I delight in looking for this short time at the features of your face, your civilian dress, and your hands, which resemble mine so much. I think if it weren't for the paralysis, I would pass my hand over your head, caress it as in other days there in our little house in La Rioja.

Although I don't know if it would stir me. You came through that door suddenly, as if you were the extension of my constant thoughts and desires. Often, when I saw you triumph, a tremor ran over my whole body. Now I don't feel my body, I see its parts as if they didn't belong to me, but when I saw you enter, I felt a kind of choking. For a moment it seemed my body was going to come alive. So I lose nothing by being paralyzed because I don't know if I'd have dared to touch you. To me you've always been something unattainable. But I know you are my nerves, my cells, and that's why I feel proud. I knew I would still see you once before I die; something told me so. And if I had been able to talk and tell you that instead of feeling it as I do, I already knew what you would have answered: Don't say that. You're going to live many years yet. That's what I said in circumstances like this. But supposing I am going to live a few more years, since our relationship is measured in years and events very far apart in time, since it's necessary for so many years to go by for me to see you, it is fair to think now that this is the last time. Even you would admit it has been so many years since we've seen one another and that time it wasn't a visit, we were together hardly fifteen minutes because you were very busy with an imminent journey. It is a way of reasoning very much yours, a product of your great intelligence, capable of demonstrating anything. Yet we must have laughed with your mother at that ability you've had since you were a child. But this time I have a very sure proof against your possible arguments, which demonstrates that we haven't seen one another for a long time and are almost two strangers: just now, involuntarily, I made the necessary sign with my eyes for doña Dora or Luisito to change my position in the chair. I have different gestures for them to set a pillow behind my head or put me to bed. They know each one. It went unnoticed by you, and that shows you haven't seen me in many years.

But this is not a reproach. I feel very happy at this moment. Now I know it's true that you have a little love for your father, and that it could not be otherwise. Doña Dora doesn't know what she says. She doesn't love you. She's half crazy. You mustn't pay any attention to what she says. But I love her very much because she is a companion to me and because she brought me here after they retired me. I don't know what would have become of me if she hadn't taken me to the pensione, because I went more than a year without drawing a cent.

But neither the years gone by nor what can be said or thought matters any longer. In the first moments of contemplation, I already felt everything had gone back in some way to the beginning because your face is as familiar as if I saw it every day; for you, my son, are the same as always, always staunch in life and ready to change the world. I am the only novelty here, with this illness of which you alone were made aware by letter. I was a little ashamed, for an instant, for you to see me in this state, but now this too seems a familiar and long-known thing.

I should have liked meeting you—wholly, as now, and on your own initiative—in earlier years, when my heart was still strong and there was promise of a long life ahead. I often sought that occasion, but it never came because the desire would have had to be mutual. But I thought then, and I think now, that you were making your own life and I had no right to interrupt it. The right moment comes a little late, when I cannot even move or communicate. I should really have liked to be able to return to our town with you one day and tell everybody This is my son. There was a woman from Santa Fe, the lead drummer's wife, who didn't believe I had a son who was a colonel. It wasn't that she didn't believe, but she looked at me as if mocking or doubting when I spoke of my son. Look, señora, this is my son, I'd say, and she'd feel ashamed and hurry for a glass to serve us a wine from the coast, and we'd drink and we'd all laugh. But anyway this meeting fulfills all my desires because at last it brings what I wanted so badly. Of course, it embarrasses me a little that my situation may make you uncomfortable. I'm very old now and actually I don't know why I would need to be moved, I don't know where I'd go. Besides, don't think I've given up. Luisito always talks about a rehabilitation center where they perform absolute miracles. It's very possible that at the end of the year I'll try it out. Perhaps we can still go back to La Rioja together someday and drink a toast with that coastal wine you yourself like.

The head drummer's wife (Bermudez's wife, you may remember him, he was a showman in the parades) always used a doubtful tone when I spoke about you. I went to their house Saturdays to eat with them, and then we played cards. That night we had finished eating and she was wiping the table with a damp rag so the cards wouldn't be stained. I had been retired for several months and things weren't going very well so they were always helping me in one way or another. During the meal I had been talking about leaving La Rioja to be nearer you (I don't remember if at the time you were in Buenos Aires or Cordoba), and she doubted that too. She refused to accept what I was saying, she treated me like an old man who doesn't know what he's saying. I told her I had a letter from Margarita, in which she let me know that if I wanted to, I could live with you. She made one of her classic faces and asked to see the letter. I didn't have it with me so I felt a little humiliated, as if there were no letter, but I told her I'd show it to her the next day. She went to the kitchen to get the cards and from there said if the letter had been from you, it would have meant something, but she put no faith in the letter from Margarita. Then, raising my voice so she'd hear, a bit annoyed by her attitude, I said if Margarita said something, it was because she relied on your approval. Then she came back and, tossing the cards onto the table, said, "Come on, don Blas, you're too old and too intelligent besides to believe such things." Bermudez made a grimace of disgust and shuffled the cards.

The woman's attitude left me upset, doubting. All through the game I was thinking you really despised me, you didn't love me, you felt ashamed of me. I had never felt anything so terrible. I was used to losing things in life, but I was not resigned to losing the only thing I had left. I remembered many of your attitudes, judging them wrongly, apart from their circumstances, and I realized that in each of them the woman was right when she said—not in words, but yes in gestures, and at times in meaningful monosyllables—not only nothing about me mattered to you, but there was even something else. That something was contempt. "But, come, don Blas, we haven't got all night," the lead drummer said, raising my spirits. That night he made a lot of signs to his wife, as if telling her that she was to blame for my frame of mind and she shouldn't say another word about those things.

I went to bed uneasy, certain that the woman was right. For many years I hadn't minded being alone, living alone, but that night I realized the house had always been deserted and I was alone. I couldn't sleep. At a single glance I could see all the events that had taken place from the time my son was born till that moment; but run together that way they told me nothing, so I began to analyze them one by one, discovering details long since forgotten.

That night was very important for me. I discovered that the woman was right, that I'd always known it, but that I had hidden it from myself, perhaps to insist it wasn't true. What she had wrong was the word, because it was not contempt you felt for me (of that you gave me several proofs), but shame. Since you were a child you've been ashamed of your father. You had begun to live in another world, you had other friendships, different tastes, and that made me glad because it meant you would have a great future. For me it was important that you have it because from the time you were very small you were timid, you had a terrible fear of the world and things. To assure your future beforehand was the best way of doing away with those fears which made you a child silent and set apart, with no friends and no love. That's why the fact that you were ashamed of your father never offended me. That's how you saved yourself from the precariousness of the small world I could offer you. And even admitting that my son despised me, as I said to the woman, what did that mean? Could I stop loving you because of your contempt? Did someone prevent my loving you as I loved you? The supposed contempt was one of your problems, which even increased my affection because it grieved me to see you suffer for a problem which, as far as I was concerned, did not exist. Your

11

contempt, if it did exist, did not stop me from loving you. And since you didn't prevent it, my love was satisfied with the sole fact that they did not prevent its existence.

Almost every afternoon, when they take me out onto the gallery, Luisito stops in front of me and says, "And now, esteemed don Blas, I'm going to act out another pantomime for you. Today's is about a servant who takes five children walking on the square." That was the last one. Using the apron as if it were a dress, he moves and walks like a woman who is trying to get someone to look at her, but the children, who play different tricks, don't let her prance about freely. When she succeeds in attracting someone's attention, she has to go running brusquely, losing all her elegance, to catch one of the children, who wants to run into the street or blow his nose or even do other indecent acts in public. He knows he can't make me laugh, at least overtly, but he must tell from my eyes that the scene amuses me. So since he doesn't need my laughter or my words to encourage his task, he transfers his shame to me. Of course, at times I do show my joy. Some pantomimes are so comical that my eyes fill with tears of pure pleasure. When he notices them, he stops acting, dries my tears with the apron, and leaves, perhaps considering the situation is too much for me. What the poor man doesn't know is that at times I neither hear nor see him because I'm very sad; and then, seeing that all his efforts to entertain me are useless, my eyes fill with tears, but of pain—for me, for my situation, and for him too. He is unaware of that hidden process, so believes I'm crying from pleasure. And if he did notice it (I believe I've sometimes seen worry on his face), it would be impossible for him to know when I am crying from grief or when I am crying for joy.

You have no children, so perhaps you don't really know the meaning of paternity. I believe having a child is very important in this life. I have been watching your features while you've been tallking to me, your eyes, your forehead, your hands, and even now, old and defeated, I feel the same thing I felt when I saw you growing up, that security and at the same time that forgetfulness which places one in the center of the world, I mean that makes one feel his own existence. The child, when born, hurts us but gives us at the same time the assurance of our own bodies, as if the open wound showed us once and for all that we had been existing and that existence itself is going. I got married somewhat late. Your mother, who lived such a short life, passed through my house like a dream and left me my son, already grown, but weak still and full of fear of the world. For me fatherhood was an event so important that it changed not only my life then but my earlier life. All that I had lived, up to that moment, came to be a fact which my memory retained only by imposition not because it had any importance. I felt, when I could call myself father, when my son was born, that my life had begun, in another way, to lack meaning, at least the meaning it had had before. I felt that my son prolonged my life a little more, saved me from the sorrows which I felt then and which were announcements of my paralysis. And I must also say that in some moments I felt being a father was a tearing apart, something related to animals, those creatures we call animals, which feel but do not seem to notice pain. No doubt, a less cruel form of prolongation in time belongs to us men, and I should have preferred to divide like amoebas, because in any case that division did not mean a rending asunder but a final and decisive action which ended then and there. When you began to grow up, I was tortured by the suffering of seeing you in the situation of permanent struggle with the hostile world which I knew too well, I saw and felt your small body and weak bones, and I was afraid of earthquakes, thieves, bats, and I don't know how many other things. I began to go to the library to read books that might help me protect you, books about diseases, work, and earth, astronomy, and in general books related to whatever surrounded you above or below, intending to protect you. That anguish fortunately soon passed. You grew, gradually acquired that expression of yours which means security and mastery of the world. Afterwards I discovered that no danger could now spy you out. Then I began to fear for myself; I suffered under the presumption that I might fail you and not help you at some moment in your life. But at the same time you were alive, articulating your first words, and at those moments I almost wanted to die, to see if with my death I made your existence more secure.

Nonetheless, that was the happiest time. Your momma, whom you resemble so much, was still alive. Separation and fear were remote things. In the first place, because, with the first cycle completed, separation seemed to have ended, and in that case the definitive act of division of the amoeba had been completed, so that all cruelty had disappeared from the smile you gave me and your mother. In the second place, fear was no longer a permanent cause because you had established all the relationships and harmonies with the world which we had given you; you had imperishable connections with buildings and months, cities and seasons. The earth's cycles were completed for you; summers succeeded winters in a perfect round in harmony with my son's life.

Afterward, your connection with the world broadened. From the perfect familiarity with the house, and even neighboring houses; with the street, whose dangers you soon learned to avoid; and with your parents, whom you learned to know, you went to primary school, to the life of relationships, and from there to the mastery of men, whose lives, as a military man, you are now used to commanding. I observed it all and felt that the sundering had not ended yet, the foreboding amoeba disappeared and returned to the long childbirth of animals under the moon, according to what I had glimpsed in I don't know what place.

But in that lapse into total happiness everything was given in plenty. My later error was searching for something similar in what remained of my life, when circumstances had changed. Of that lapse I can say it is like that inviolate part of infancy which one usually remembers, where there is nothing, not even memories, which can alter that pure passing. My infancy lay in you, in yours, and no one can take that away from me, neither the lead drummer's wife nor my son's contempt or shame. It was the time when I caressed you. You were my son, you had no defenses, I looked after you desperately; my son loved me too in his innocence; he looked at me, laughed, stretched his arms out to me, sought my protection. Then things changed. He began to be ashamed of me, the old man. Of course, years had gone by.

I wouldn't have liked remembering the matter of the letters, but just now, while you were talking to me, trying to adapt the meaning and subject of your words to a listener who could answer nothing, referring to events and things which you think may interest me, you made several mistakes which show me that most of the letters were not read. Margarita had already told me that, years before. "Dad, it's better not to write so many letters. At times we're not at home for several months, and when we return, Victor finds he has so many letters from you that he puts off reading them and finally many letters go unread." Margarita didn't tell the truth either, because you were never away so many months. I know too, from Olga, that important letters were forwarded. I realize I wrote too much. I did it on those nights of such frequent insomnia. At times I wrote two letters in a single night, but I sent them a week or two apart. I didn't expect answers. I made that clear in many letters. I wrote only because I needed to, because I believed I had to tell you things you should know. In some letters, certainly, I reproached you for your lack of love, your indifference; I complained because I believed my son did not love me. I understood that this annoyed you, like when "I spied on you," as you violently told me, but I couldn't avoid it. That day you insulted me for the first time; you said, among other things, I should be thankful I'm your father because otherwise your attitude would have been far different. I think that night you might have hit me. There was such hate in your look. It was after the episode in the men's room, which I'm ashamed of, when you stepped over me while I was down on the floor looking for my glasses, thinking I hadn't seen you. Possibly when you insulted me, you got rid of the fury caused by the episode in the men's room. You left a nightclub with other people, undoubtedly military, although all in civilian dress. It was very late. I had taken a walk downtown because of my insomnia. It wasn't that I had gone looking for you there; they had simply told me you frequented that place, and I went near the door on the chance I'd see you. That's all. I wasn't even going to speak if I saw you. For many months I hadn't been able to find you at home, and I couldn't miss the chance of seeing you and feeling consoled by such a simple act. You, when you saw me, didn't give me time to slip away as at other times in other places, and, clutching your head, you insulted I don't know whom with all your fury. Did you believe I'd tell Margarita you came out of a place like that with another woman? If you thought that, it was because you didn't know your father very well. Your insult was so emphatic that your friends stopped to ask you what had happened. I was standing against the wall, terrified by what I had done. Suddenly you jerked your hands from your head and, pointing, your arm thrust out at me, you said to your friends, "That son of a bitch is my father." I swear to you it was like a knife in me. Luckily the effect your words were having on me, the humiliation and shame I began to feel (not at the words but because you had said them) were interrupted and gave way to the fear caused by seeing you come toward me, take me by the lapels and slam me against the wall. Your friends took you by the arms and freed me. Otherwise perhaps you'd have beaten me up. No doubt you were about to say something else to me, but the policeman, whom you also badly insulted when he came to ask you what was happening, prevented it. One of your friends took out his military ID and showed it to the policeman and at once you all got into the auto. I was straightening out my clothes. The policeman murmured something, and when I approached to say something to him, because I was terribly ashamed, he said what perhaps you would have said if he hadn't interrupted: "And you—get out of here once and for all. Beat it right now." The automobile had disappeared by the time I really heard or finished hearing his insult. They were hard words, which had suddenly transformed you and, in a certain way, me. But I'd no sooner heard the words than a part of me hid them in a very secret place so I could forget them, so I in some way wouldn't find that place.

Never would I have told you this, son. I kept it in that unknown part which does not belong to me, and it has never left that place. Nor could I say you made me suffer. I understood you. And a proof of how right I was is that kiss you just gave me when you came in. Had I hung onto that earlier event, you'd have shown me now that I was wrong.

That night, after leaving the lead drummer's house, I remembered all this and much more. If she hadn't said to me, "Come now, don Blas, I'm surprised that you still believe certain things," referring to the help you'd have given me and making your possible affection doubtful, perhaps those memories would have remained in that secret place where I'm used to keeping things which can hurt me. The ugly side of the matter is that after the memory of each episode came another one, worse. I decided to bring it all out in the open to get rid of it all, so the next day I would confront the lead drummer's wife and defend my son.

And the result was excellent. The candid part of me said it was dangerous to dredge from my secret part the things I'd always feared: it could mean beating my head against the wall. But the woman's voice, which had then come from the kitchen to the table where I was sitting, came to me now in bed and demanded that I do it. I opened that door with great fear. Once, when I was very young, I discovered something in the rear patio and forgot the matter. An aunt of mine used to have nocturnal visions and cried out in the middle of the night, asking them to help her and protect her from certain creatures which came to devour her while she was sleeping. We looked for the strange things in every possible hiding place, but with no luck. I remember I tore the canvas over the attic hole with a long stick and poked inside until I touched the corners, but the things did not appear. Then somebody told my aunt that by burying I don't know what very strange objects inside a bottle, at the end of the patio, the creatures would disappear and she would sleep peacefully. My aunt made fun of the advice, but I carried it out. In a room out back, full of all kinds of objects, I looked for God knows what and put them in a bottle, which I buried. I forgot the matter completely, and sometime after I remembered and began to look for the place where the bottle might be, but full of doubt because in the long run I didn't know if it had really happened or I'd dreamed it.

The point is that I found the bottle and at the moment of opening it I was very afraid because I didn't know what horrible things I'd put in it. I then opened the part of me where oblivion and also memory lay, and I let the things out. At that moment I seemed to see that from the bottom of the bottle came some enormous black birds with red eyes which stared at me, perhaps the same birds my aunt had seen.

One of the things which came out of the bottle was the comet. Until then, when my son denied anything I said, his denial made me glad at heart: He's a man, I thought. But at the matter of the comet I was somewhat saddened for the first time, because it seemed to me he believed none of the things I said. And it grieved me also because when I talked about the comet, I did so handing on to him facts, knowledge which I had looked up in the library precisely for him when I wanted to protect him from everything which surrounded him and sought laboriously in books (many of them recommended by the lead drummer; I remember the beautiful bound volumes of Reclus's *The Earth*, which had such an aura of mystery), among such a quantity of books, security for that face I had thrust into the world. I was already used to the fact that everything I did or said was a mistake or defect, but the comet I hadn't invented; wise men who had spent their lives studying the facts wrote of the comet. It was an extremely calm night. You were already asleep—I think it was very late. I had been copying musical scores. Through the window Vargas, the cornetist, stuck his head and asked if I'd seen the comet. He seemed frightened. I had heard about it, but I had not seen it yet. I went out to the patio and there it was in the middle of the sky, with its head and its immense tail giving off fire. I watched it an instant and smiled, filled with an immense joy. Something I had read in lifeless print was there, demonstrating truth. I intended to go wake you immediately to show you that wonder and show you that what I had told you about comets was true, but Vargas, quite excited, didn't stop talking, relating country superstitions filled with terrors. It was evident he didn't believe what he was saying, but the subject delighted him. I half-listened because I began to think how afraid of stars you were. The first time you saw them consciously you were afraid they'd fall down on you. Everything I could explain to you about that impossibility was useless. When you didn't understand a thing, you scowled, shut your eyes tight, and said, "It can't be," and then refused to go on talking about the matter. One time, you didn't want to accept the Earth's forming part of the Milky Way. It was one of your father's many mistakes. The cornetist soon forgot the comet and went on talking about other things. When I stopped thinking about the matter of the Milky Way and listened attentively again, he was talking about the salaries they had promised us and the possibility that the legislature would not approve the new tax because there was feeling against it among the representatives. Happily, he left and I hurried to your room. "Son, come see the comet," I said. You didn't hear me very well, you let me take you and dress you, but when we got to the patio and you opened your eyes and saw that ball of fire in the sky, you looked at me as if terrified. There was a neighboring cornfield which could be seen almost as if it were daylight. Nearby the cocks were crowing, and the dogs were barking in the distance. You asked me to put you down. When I did so, you looked toward the comet and in your expression there was, I believe a flash of acceptance. You looked at me as if telling me you were surprised to verify what you had once believed to be legend or error in your father's mouth. I felt proud. You asked me several questions which I answered rapidly. Do you remember? Mane. Tail. I knew many things about comets. That grimace of doubt came over your face when I stated that the comet would return to Earth in seventy-six years. I said you would see it again and that was a real piece of luck because many people went through life without being able to see a comet. You went to bed right away. Your mother was anxious to put you back in bed as if she too feared the comet. I stayed up a while watching until it began to fade. Then I went to bed thinking that the permanent disbelief you had about everything must be something fundamental, some primary confidence, but I failed to imagine what it could be. I was afraid it might be something dangerous. Afterwards I fell asleep with an answer which earlier, referring to other events, the lead drummer had given me: your denials were nothing more than forms of your security, they were demonstrations that you were already a man. The next day, when you got up, I was in the patio and, pointing a finger at the sky, I said as soon as I saw you, "The street of the comet." You didn't look up, but it seems you smiled. I was very satisfied that day.

That night while I was remembering the comet, I couldn't get out of my head the face of the lead drummer's wife when she'd told me I was too old to go on believing in certain things. If I told her about the comet, no doubt she'd have used the same expression of triumph or certainty like telling me that that was one more proof of my son's feelings toward me. The truth is she humiliated me a little; but still there was much more to it and I must get to the bottom of my shame in order to know, according to what I'd glimpsed, that all that was nothing, that my face, my form, *father*, and his face, his form, *son*, still endured and that the life relationship was indestructible despite all there might be inside the bottle.

Because one is only his own irreplaceable form, with his nose, which can be a beautiful memory, his ears, the cut of his face, like those caricatures some people make. Once they made one of me. "Yes, that's me," I had to admit when I looked at it, because it couldn't be anybody but me. One is only his form, which limits him to the rest of the world. Inside are the viscera and all the rest, but one is finally that, the oval of the head, the total form barely constricted into the neck, eyes, arms which fake sinuosities and then straight lines toward the ground, terminating in still tips which are displaced by the earth. One is finally a form which contains a single life and a single death. One is a kind of jail in which he is condemned to live and die. But there is something which saves him when he imagines the total existence of another being (his form and what it contains) and feels suddenly that that other being responds, and then those forms, touched by love, unite and feel they are no longer single forms, single jails, but share the wondrous world. When one has felt that, when one has felt touched by that vision of forms which is called love, then what do death and oblivion matter, what does all the rest matter if in some way he feels that all the other beings are responding for one, are affirming the precariousness of their own limitations. For that reason, discovering now that you love me, I feel, son, that my life is totally fulfilled. So it is beautiful to be alive to feel that all the beings in the world—those who are near, even those one doesn't know, and those who are in other latitudes—respond to one, accompany him in the world, are with him to assure him of his own existence. I can tell you that it has been beautiful to be alive and that I am thankful for having been able to live in this form and in this world.

That night I had wanted to go rapidly over the events of your childhood to bring to light other, more recent and painful events and master them as quickly as possible, but my glance into time lingered too long and I had to consider others, as if the comet itself had illuminated them. If I had not remembered the comet, perhaps those other tangential events would have remained in forgetfulness. And seeking some blame, some act which had hurt my son, I remembered that twenty-fifth of May, the parade in which my son was standard-bearer and suffered because I didn't want to go see him in the parade. Your mother and you reproached me severely the next day. I was silent. And all that I kept silent within me, I said to myself then before the memory of the stern face of the lead drummer's wife, as if she demanded it of me. I remembered then that before that twenty-fifth of May there was another. The square was full of people and soldiers. The military mass had ended and the white rows of students converged on the flag to render their homage. Your mother and I tried to locate the place your school would occupy. We were on the corner by the cathedral. In those years I was afraid of time; I mean, I was afraid that time would pass. La Rioja is surrounded by mountains, it is small and there everybody knows everybody else. The familiar and identical faces and the near mountains always gave me the sensation of confinement. I was brought up on the plains, where one is always free. There, among the mountains and the repetitive faces, I felt time go by quickly, I felt it hurt us day after day. I had begun to discover I don't know what horrible adult form in your young face. The schools had begun the procession and I was looking at those thousands of faces among which yours would later appear. Hundreds of faces passed before me, dark, red, white, and all of them, the order of march from youngest to oldest, indicated that time had passed and went on passing. When it was your school's turn, you went by without looking at us. No doubt any least distraction would break the solemnity of the event. We respected the importance you gave to such things as parades and patriotic emblems. For us they had no importance but we accepted them because they had our son's reverence. You were the flag escort. Your mother and I noticed, besides the solemnity of your action, that your face seemed tormented. That morning, while you were dressing, you said something which made us understand you were disgusted because you'd have liked being the standard-bearer but were only the escort. You were the most martial. My eyes filled with tears, your mother's did too. I don't know why she was crying, but I did know why I was: because time had passed, because you had become a man, little one, who suddenly had to confront the world with the stars on high and the endless round of seasons and all the dangers of the world. Among thousands, your face had passed; it was something I had given to mankind: a face, a form. I did not turn to see your back. I kept looking at the other faces, adults too in endless repetition. Then I saw that your mother had turned to watch you from behind. I remember well your mother's profile against the sun. The voice over the loudspeaker was now announcing the passing of the next school before the official stand—the industrial school, "the country's reserve," according to the speaker. For that reason I didn't want to go to the parade the following year, when you had become standard-bearer. While you were dressing, with that fastidiousness of yours, you didn't show that being standard-bearer delighted you. I said so to your mother and she said yes you were happy, but that your face showed displeasure because you knew I wouldn't go to the parade. I'd like to have explained my reasons to you, but I was ashamed to. When I tried to kiss you good-bye you turned your face away. But I didn't ascribe that action to your momentary anger because at other times you had turned your face away when I tried to kiss you. That was simply part of your character, so I didn't believe, contrary to your mother's fears, that you were upset with me because I wasn't going to the parade. Besides, if I had said, "Son, I'm not going because I'm afraid of time passing," you'd really have been offended. But that night I realized that your mother was right. You didn't come home to supper or join us afterward to see the fireworks as we had agreed. When you later opened the front door—from the house you could hear the explosions of the fireworks which were beginning—and saw I was waiting for you in the front room, you turned to the corridor and went into the kitchen. You went straight to bed. In a while I went to your bed to say good night. You didn't answer, though you were awake. I felt a great humiliation, shame, something like that. I wanted to kneel and ask your forgiveness. I believe that night I began to suffer the insomnia which since, with age, came to be more frequent and longer. I couldn't sleep. I got up and went out to the garden. I leaned against the fence and saw high in the sky one of those fireworks. It resembled a quick comet. I remembered that night years back, when you were very young and, wrapped in a blanket, your body nestled against mine because you were afraid of the unfamiliar fire.

If it hadn't been for that woman's attitude, I'd never have dredged all those things out of myself. Never would I have said them to anyone, not even my son, and if he himself had demanded I tell them, I'd have refused, saying those things were absolutely mine and therefore would remain inside me. The truth is that I remembered some and dwelled on the details, on lapses of time, and beyond them I spied hundreds of similar things. And to alleviate that shame which remembering them caused me, the aggression they signified, I recalled instead others in which no doubt I was primarily to blame, so as to tell the woman afterward that you really had reasons to be ashamed of me. Then I remembered the incident in the men's room, painful because it happened in silence on both sides. Seeing it clearly, the insult at the nightclub was preferable to the terrible silence of that night.

We had seen each other for a few minutes, several days before. You were getting ready for a trip and gave me the money to return to La Rioja. I didn't go back but went to a friend's house. I was anxious to see you, that's all, and I don't know how I learned you were attending a banquet in a downtown hotel. I think I saw the news in the paper. I knew you had the obsession that I followed you, spied on you, so I was very careful that night. I simply wanted to see what that meal was like, how you shone among so many distinguished people. I entered through the employees' entrance and hid in the men's room. From there I could see you perfectly. The table was immense and there were many officers with their wives. Margarita was one of the most beautiful. They were laughing and eating. The men's room was perfect to see from. Only two officers came in during more than half an hour, to urinate and comb their hair. One said, "What's wrong, old boy?" I said I was perfectly all right. Then I amused myself listening to an argument between two waiters and I didn't notice that you had gotten up and were coming to the men's room. You walked with quick, determined steps, with a serious expression very different from the almost permanent smile you wore at the table. I hit on the idea of taking my glasses off and dropping them on the floor and kneeling to look for them. When you opened the door, it struck my shoe. I looked up as if to explain I'd gone in there by chance and was looking for my glasses, but I couldn't say a word. You looked at me angrily and I remembered many things. For a moment I was afraid, but you raised one foot, then another and stepped over me, and I kept looking for my glasses. We were both pretending we didn't see one another. When I tried to leave, I had bad luck—the service entrance was closed at that hour, so I had to cross the dining room, where you were all eating. Clinging close to the wall, I walked with fear and shame. I think there was a mirror on the wall; and although I didn't look at myself in it, I knew I was out of place there. The lights grew brighter and brighter as I neared the exit. Margarita saw me too, I'm sure. I couldn't avoid her eyes being directed toward the wall I was edging slowly along, bent so that at least some wouldn't see me. When I reached the door the porter looked at me surprised. I smiled, with effort I kept the smile on my face until I was out of the porter's gaze; then I felt the muscles in my face as heavy as if my cheeks had been about to fall. I decided to go back to La Rioja that very night, but I was aware that I hadn't enough for the fare since I'd spent some. I could ask my friend, but I hadn't the heart to. But actually I was thinking of returning and all that so as not to think of the humiliation I was experiencing, the blame which caused me such anguish. The worst thing of all was that you hadn't said a thing to me, that you hadn't at least insulted me. I felt we were two strangers and there was no longer any possible contact between us. I realized then that all my attitude toward you was only imbecility, ridiculousness. But I couldn't avoid that because I wanted to see you, I needed to be near you, to have some form of communication. If to that inevitable necessity on my part the absurdity or ridiculousness were added, the result was the certainty that you were already for me a lost cause. That night I ended up in a tavern. Some boys bought me a couple of drinks. I recited them a good bit of *Martin Fierro* by heart.

I don't know what you could be saying to Luis now. I paid no attention to the beginning of the conversation, and now your words make no sense. At first I understood everything. You were asking Luis things about me, and he answered others, because what you were asking didn't apply to my situation. Then he tried to ask you how one communicated with me and he said several times, "Come, don Blas, now tell me if you want me to put you to bed. Well, don Blas, if you want me to take you to the bathroom," waiting for me to move my eyes to one side or the other, but I didn't want to do it, I didn't want my son to know how these things are done. And if you stay until dinnertime I'm going to be awfully ashamed for you to know how they feed your father, the man who knew so many things.

Everything comes in due time. Forced prostration has brought me almost to the doors of wisdom (imagine what wisdom must mean to me). I am no longer impatient, and if I had been able to think this way before, I'd never have followed you through so many streets and cities. Besides, it is through waiting that desire matures. It is good to see the day unfurl, feel the movement of the Earth like something which is happening intimately. The seasons, once feared, are now the very existence of one who feigns beautiful changes. Memories themselves are a form of permanence, life arrested, not buried, which is always within hand's reach, which is always a new possibility of living. When I was a young father and you an indifferent son, your coldness made me despair. You never performed spontaneous acts of affection and hardly accepted my own. That time I was sick you came into my room twice, but said nothing. When the doctor left and our fears vanished, your mother, joyful, embraced me in bed and wept against me. "I was afraid something awful had happened to you," she said. After, she got up and in her great happiness said, "Victor, come hug your father because he's all right, he's not sick." You came in shortly after and stood beside my bed. It was an embarrassing situation for us both. I felt like somebody who had deliberately hurt himself to get protection. You hesitated, I don't know what you must have felt, and because you hesitated so long, I extended my arms and said, "Come, son, give your father a hug," feeling, shamefully, that I was begging an action of love which otherwise might not have come. You climbed up on my bed, first let me hug you and then you yourself hugged me. But you didn't give me the kiss I expected. That attitude of yours was the cause, for years, of secret shames. That lost kiss came now, all these years later, as if it had been seeking until now the perfect moment of maturation. What good, then, is impatience? The adult son who kissed me just now is the same son who had no desire to bend over my bed when I was sick. I understand now that your mother was right: "It isn't that he doesn't love you; that's the way he is." But I needed a lifetime to realize that. Luckily, meanwhile my desire has ripened into possession.

All those things I thought about in bed, tossing and turning as if to run from some of them. Suddenly I remembered I hadn't looked for Margarita's letter in which she invited me to spend a few days with you both and which I had promised to the lead drummer's wife. I got up and went through some cabinets, but I realized it would be very hard to find because it was a very old letter. To go back without the letter was shameful, so I decided to write one in which I told myself that you and Margarita wanted me to live with you because I was old and mustn't be in La Rioja going without. I recognize that it was a shameful act. Afterward I leaned against the fence, looking at the sky and again I remembered the comet. Above, there was a perfectly formed path along which the comet, full of fire, would pass many years later when my son would be as old as I then was. And now it no longer grieved me that time had passed, as it did that time at the parade. I had begun to understand the ultimate truth of things.

The vision of the comet's path made me stop continuing to pull things out of those dark deeps in me Your absence was very long but your return so certain that I was ashamed of the smallness of my actions. I tore up the letter I'd written myself to show my friend's wife. Neither the letter nor the woman herself was important any longer.

I went to bed again, determined to think no more about all that, but the black birds kept emerging from the depths of the bottle. The action of my will kept many inside, but I couldn't stop watching those already in flight. Some of those birds were Lanús, Liniers, Pompeya, Buenos Aires. At that period you were the follower. I rented cheap rooms in one place and another (I had a woman), trying to hide from you so you wouldn't find out about my poverty. But at times I'd come home and my neighbors would say, "Some military man was here. He left this card." I had to go see you then and you reproached me for "the scandalous life" I was leading. Another time you sent two soldiers to fumigate my room. They took my papers and clothes and burned everything in the patio. You told me it was because of the filth so you'd ordered them to burn it all. But among them were papers valuable to me, photographs, souvenirs, newspaper clippings, documents. My companion and I decided then to move, but your soldiers always arrived and harassed us, or you appeared and left those cards. After that the revolts began and you stopped following us. You appeared in the newspapers. When my neighbors and friends heard me say I was your father many of them laughed at me, but many others believed it. Finally we went to live in Boedo, where we rented a garage. There my woman died and I went back to Cordoba, where doña Dora took me in. Then came my illness and with it my lucidity, my understanding of so many things.

But the day after that night I went back to the lead drummer's house. We had played three hands of truco when the woman asked me about the letter. I played the fool, answering half in truth, half in jest, telling her in a little while I'd pull it out of my inside pocket. I loved making her laugh, acting out different personalities and disguising my voice. She was very simple and laughed at anything provided I said it. Then I talked like a circus magician when he announces he's going to pull something out of the bottom of his hat. In five minutes, I said, I m going to pull three letters from my pocket. After, gradually, I arranged them so I could talk about the comet. The woman opened her enormous eyes. I invented such stories about the comet that she was amazed for the rest of the night. Then I slipped away, under the moon, smoking a cigar the lead drummer had given me.

They were very good people. He was from Malanzán. In summer they invited me to share their fruit. Try them, don Blas, these are peaches from Malanzán, she'd say. He had a little house there, with an orchard, and every year he received crates of fruit. I remember him especially for the fall he took one day. A military government had taken over the province, and we had to march and play. I came with the drums, after the cornets, but I could see him perfectly, at the head of the column, making pirouettes in the air with his baton. He handled it very well. When he reached the corner by the bank, they ordered a right flank and he tried to change hands, flinging the baton into the air, but it fell a couple of yards away, and he went down on all fours a few yards from the official stand where the military inspector was. A lot of people burst into laughter. He never mentioned the matter. Afterward he raised the baton in the most dignified way possible and continued brandishing it with even greater skill as if nothing had happened. Later he received a serious dressing down.

It seems, son, you want to leave and are trying to hit on a strategic exit so I won't be upset. Luis has suggested leaving, it seems, and that shows he doesn't know me as he should either. Your leaving won't affect me as they think. I've come to an understanding of many things. I've seen you, I've heard you, I've received the kiss postponed since your childhood, and my desires have been satisfied. From now on, although I may not see you again, I shall be able to spend many hours and days in the contemplation and renewed enjoyment of this meeting. Everything has happened so quickly, you arrived so unexpectedly, that I shall need a lot of time to assimilate so many really beautiful things. I shall look at that threshold and tell myself you came through it and sat in that chair looking at me and talking to me although I heard very little you said. I don't perceive words now, but attitudes. Those are what are worthwhile. I see you restless, anxious to leave. Perhaps this causes you pain. You don't know how to leave so you seek Luis's help. I myself turn to him for help. Although I'd like to keep you here forever, I know that's not possible. You have to go on living your life to fulfill a great destiny. You must see the comet. Right away, when Luis looks at me, I make my eyes move so he understands I am tired and want him to put me to bed. But first I'll do one thing: I'll indicate to him that I want you yourself to take me. It will be like giving you back the kiss you've given me.

Luis understood the sign for changing places perfectly, but he had a little difficulty capturing my desire that you move me. You smile with a flash of your mother in your eyes and lift me in your arms. Now my cup is filled to overflowing, every hope ended. As if you were my father, I feel like a child again, needing affection.

Now I'd like you to go as quickly as possible. At once they'll have to relieve me, wash and prepare me for supper, and I don't want you to experience these things. I'll give Luis instructions to hand on to you my drum, which earned me my living. Lately, I've been quite doubled up. I don't want you to carry away a painful image of your father. I know I'm not worthy of you, but I don't want your memory of me to be more disagreeable than my condition. I would like you, in the many years you have left to live, to remember me as a man who could talk to you with precision about comets and the movement of the stars.

Daniel Moyano, author of several prize-winning stories, was born in 1930 in Buenos Aires. He was provincial correspondent for the province of La Rioja, on the daily Clarin *of Buenos Aires, before going into self-exile to Madrid. In 1986 he received the coveted Juan Rulfo Award in Mexico. Famous in Argentina, and gaining renown in other countries, his work is published in several languages. H.E. Francis, his friend and translator of this story, is a talented short story writer, as well as a translator and university professor.*

"They want to punish me because I did my duty."

Within Four Walls

BY STEPHEN KELEN

NORTON, the male nurse, brought the new patient into Doctor Solugbov's office.

"This is a special case, Doc," he said with the intimacy that exists between people who work together under strained circumstances.

"I know," agreed Doctor Solugbov with a deep sigh. A cold shiver ran through his body. He dreaded seeing the gaunt, emaciated-looking patient.

"This bloke," Norton continued his carefree chatter, "hardly speaks English. Well, that's what he says, anyway. In any case, he'll be more at home with you, Doc."

"Yes," Solugbov agreed bitterly, "he'll be more at home with me."

The new patient at first stood at rigid attention, but now he started to tremble. He slowly lifted a shaky left arm and covered his face. His desperate gestures strangely terrified Solugbov.

"I must not be afraid of him," he said to himself. "He cannot harm me now. I'm in Australia...in Australia." Then, speaking with difficulty, he said aloud: "You'd better leave us alone, Norton. Wait outside. I'll ring for you."

"O.K., Doc. I don't think he's dangerous. He is frightened of something I guess. I have never seen a man more cowed than this one."

As soon as Norton left the room Solugbov felt regret and fear. With uncertain hands he poured himself a glass of water. Then he turned to his patient, and said in Bulgarian: "Sit down, please. You don't have to be afraid of anything here. I am your doctor, my only aim is to help you."

The patient sank into the chair. The sound of his native tongue calmed him. He leaned towards Solugbov, and whispered: "It is good to hear Bulgarian. You...you speak like one of us...Where did you learn our language?"

"In Sofia," Dr. Solugbov said, and felt easier now. "You see, I'm a Bulgarian, too."

"Thank goodness for that," the patient sighed. "I'll be able to speak to you freely."

"Of course," Solugbov tried to reassure him.

"They are after me, Doctor Solugbov; they want to kill me...I can't sleep...I can't eat...They might poison my food...One of their men followed me all day yesterday...I just couldn't put up with it any longer...Please, Doctor Solugbov, please...Don't let them kill me."

"I don't think anyone wants to kill you." Solugbov forced himself to speak calmly.

"But they do," the man insisted. "I know they do."

Solugbov knew that this was the moment when he had to ask his patient the vital question that would open the gate to his distorted mind.

"And who are they?" he asked.

"The Jews, of course. I'm Colonel Zacharoff. I was the commandant of a concentration camp in Sofia. They know about me. They want to punish me because I did my duty."

"Don't worry, Colonel Zacharoff. No harm will come to you. I

31

will personally see to that." Solugbov's voice was rising to a high pitch.

"Thank you, thank you." Colonel Zacharoff expressed his gratitude effusively.

Solugbov rang the bell. Norton came in and took the patient away.

Doctor Solugbov sat at his desk, dazzled by this sudden interlude, which brought back to him all the horrors of the concentration camp, the pogroms he and his people had to suffer.

Without knowing it consciously, he started to cry. He was sobbing softly just as he did when he saw his beloved people dying, perishing in Colonel Zacharoff's infamous concentration camp.

Doctor Gordon came into the room. He sat on the same chair Colonel Zacharoff had occupied a few minutes before.

"Your eyes are bloodshot, Louis," Gordon remarked innocently. "This darned light in here. You'd better ask for stronger globes, or a special fitting."

"There's nothing wrong with my eyes, John," Doctor Solugbov said, much to his own amazement. "I was crying."

"Crying? You'd better have a long holiday, old man; your nerves must be on edge. We all have an occasional crack-up in this game. If you like, I can speak to the old man."

"Thank you, John, thank you very much." A warm tide of gratitude overwhelmed Solugbov. He felt better now. "Believe me, my nerves are all right. I don't need a holiday, I just have to face up to a terrible ghost from my past."

"A ghost from your past?"

"Yes, a ghost from my past. A few minutes ago they brought in Colonel Zacharoff. He was a notorious Jew baiter in Bulgaria. He was responsible for the death of thousands of Jews; my family was among his victims. I was one of his prisoners, but he doesn't recognize me now. He is afraid that the Jews are going to take revenge on him."

"I'm sorry, Louis. They shouldn't have brought him to you. If you like I can take him over. Or we may send him to another asylum."

"I'm afraid that's impossible," Solugbov said resignedly. "You see, he can speak hardly any English."

"Well, that doesn't really matter. We have doctors who speak German, Rumanian, Hungarian and many other tongues."

Doctor Solugov laughed bitterly.

"Yes, we have doctors who speak all kind of languages, but Colonel Zacharoff doesn't. He was such a patriot, Colonel Zacharoff was, that he refused to learn any other tongue but his own."

"What are you going to do then?"

"I have no choice, John. I must do my duty."

No sooner had he said "duty" than a fearful doubt formed in Solugbov's mind. "Just what is my duty?" he asked himself. "Am I to attempt to cure this monster and let him go free? It is quite clear that he is not an incurable case. His papers state that he suffers from a persecution complex, but they don't say anything about his past. Supposing I report him to the authorities? They will send him back to Europe, a most fertile ground for his activities! If I say nothing and he is discharged and allowed to live in Australia, then, yes, I will have betrayed my adopted country, because he will work to spread the slow, horrible poison of planned hatred among Australians."

"Well, I guess"—he heard Doctor Gordon's voice—"there's nothing else for us but to do our duty. If I may say so, Louis, I admire you for your attitude."

That night Doctor Solugbov had a strange, but quite explainable dream. He was wearily trudging along a seemingly endless road. In the distance, through the semi-darkness he could see on top of a hill the silhouettes of three crucifixes. He felt terribly tired. All he wanted was to rest, rest forever. Just as he was going to sit down at the wayside, a gentle voice whispered into his ear. "To discover the truth you must go the distance, my friend." With a desperate effort he forced himself to continue his journey.

At long last he arrived at his destination. What he saw made him cry out in despair. His wife and son were crucified on two crosses. He wanted to rush and free them, but just then Norton, the Asylum orderly came to him. He was leading Colonel Zacharoff on a chain.

"Excuse me, sir," Norton said. "The cross in the center, as you see, is still vacant. You must decide yourself whether this man, or you yourself are to be crucified. The decision, sir, rests entirely with you."

With a loud cry Doctor Solugbov woke up. The pale light of dawn filtered through the drawn blinds. Hurriedly he dressed himself. He had an insane desire to see Colonel Zacharoff right away. There was a crazy urge in him to reveal his true identity to this tormentor who had followed him to this farthest part of the Earth. "God has delivered him into my hands," he said. With trembling hands he searched in his medicine chest for the hypodermic...Just then there was a loud knock on the door. Hurriedly he turned around.

"Come in," he cried out.

Norton entered. His usually calm countenance expressed alarm.

"Doctor Solugbov," he muttered, "the Bulgarian..."

"Yes, the Bulgarian?"

"It was all my fault, I guess." Norton went on. "But how was I to know?"

"Know what?"

"You see, when I took the Bulgarian back to his room I said to him...I said to him probably he had to suffer in a concentration camp, just like you did. He understood me all right, because he asked: 'Doctor Solugbov in concentration camp?' 'Yes,' I said. 'The Bulgarian Nazis put him in a concentration camp, because he was a Jew.'"

"And?"

"He didn't answer. I took him back to his room. A few minutes later I met Doctor Gordon who told me about your problem. I thought it was pretty tough, but forgot all about your patient...Until this morning..."

"Yes, yes. What happened this morning?"

"I went to see him on my round...and found him in a pool of blood. He bit his veins open. There was a note at his side. Here. I can't read it."

Doctor Solugbov took the piece of paper and in nervous haste read the Cyrillic letters: GOD FORGIVE THOSE WHO SIN AGAINST THEIR

FELLOW MEN.

Deep remorse, and, at the same time, an unearthly happiness filled Solugbov.

"Did you take him to the hospital?" he asked. "We must save him at all costs. We must not let him die."

"I'm afraid its too late," said Norton. "The man is dead."

 *Stephen Kelen, an Australian by choice, was born in Budapest and educated there and at Prague University. His short stories, poems and articles have been published since he was seventeen. He is also a playwright and the author of several novels. He wrote first in Hungarian, then in Czech and now writes in English. He has traveled the world and been published in many countries. He is a member of several professional associations, among them the Australian Journalists Association, Australian Society of Authors, and the International PEN Sydney Center of which he was president from 1975 to 1985. In 1986 he was awarded the OAM (Medal of the Order of Australia) for his service to literature.*

"The closer they got to home, memories crowded into his mind with aching clarity."

A Flying Visit

BY ERIC CAMERON

AFTER moving around the world for more than ten years, Larry Hagen expected to see the little town changed, but progress seemed to have overlooked Riverdale. Driving along the single business street was like traveling back into his past.

"Not so fast, Mulligan," he said to the burly, gray-haired man at the wheel. "You're liable to get a ticket."

Mulligan chuckled and when Larry glanced at the other man sharing the back seat with him, Harris also smiled slightly. He was younger than Larry and Mulligan. He had been studying a road map, using his briefcase as a table. Now he put the map away and his pale blue eyes glanced from side to side, taking in every detail.

"Want to pay a courtesy call on the mayor?" Mulligan asked, a glint of amusement flickering in his usually impassive gray eyes that could be as hard as granite.

"I don't even know who he is," Larry replied. "The last time I came home was nine years ago and that was just for a weekend."

"You never do stay long in one place," Harris remarked.

"Foot-loose and fancy-free, that's me," Larry said lightly. But seeing the familiar landmarks, like the old red brick bank building, had triggered memories that gave the moment a tinge of sadness.

They passed the cemetery which seemed larger than Larry remembered, the tombstones very white among the somber evergreens. Three miles out of town Larry told Mulligan to turn down a secondary road that followed the river, then wound into the rolling hills, hazy in the distance. The foliage on the riverbank was a blaze of color...scarlet and tarnished gold tinged with purple and brown. Its beauty was all the more poignant because it was so transient. Larry remembered hunting in the hills with his father on autumn days like this, the stillness of the woods shrouding everything like a soft blanket. The closer they got to home, memories crowded into his mind with aching clarity.

"It's the next place on the left," he told Mulligan.

"Nice view," Harris said as the car slowed to turn into the gravel drive.

An old man was raking dead leaves on the lawn in front of the white clapboard house. Larry swallowed hard and for a fleeting moment considered telling Mulligan to drive on. As they got out of the car the man peered near-sightedly. Then he approached, walking stiffly, and Larry knew that rheumatism was taking its toll of the strong legs and back. He wore an old tweed jacket and a battered felt hat with several tattered trout flies hooked into the discolored band.

"Don't forget we can't stay long," Harris reminded Larry.

As Ben Hagen came closer his smile suddenly widened with recognition. He grabbed Larry's hand and squeezed it in a grip that still had a trace of its one-time strength. His eyes glistened and Larry suddenly experienced the same surge of emotion that made speech difficult.

"It's been a long time," Ben Hagen said in a husky voice.

Larry nodded and swallowed hard before he introduced his companions. "Paul Mulligan and Bruce Harris. We're on a business trip, but I managed to coax them to drive out of the way just so I could say hello."

His father's face clouded. "You're not staying?"

"Wish I could," Larry said, "but there's a very important meeting tonight."

"We just couldn't have it without him," Harris added.

"It's just as if you dropped out of the sky," the old man said, taking in the cut of Larry's expensive business suit.

"That's just about the way of it, Mr. Hagen," Mulligan said. "We met Larry when he got off the plane from South America last night."

"All the flights this morning were grounded by fog," Larry added. "That's why we had to drive."

Ben Hagen nodded. "There's always heavy morning fog when you get a spell of warm days and cool nights. C'mon, let's go inside."

A delicious aroma of baking filled the house and Judith Hagen came out of the kitchen with a smudge of flour on her forehead. When she recognized Larry her smile froze and her eyes opened wide. Then she was in his arms, laughing and sobbing and leaving dusty flour marks where she patted the back of his dark jacket.

"Oh, I do look a mess," she said as she dabbed at her eyes with a corner of her blue polka-dot apron.

"You look wonderful," Larry insisted.

"I can hardly believe it's Larry," she said to Ben for the third time. "After all these years."

After introducing the others, Larry explained in quick, terse sentences how the unexpected visit had come about. When his mother heard how brief it must be, the look of dismay in her eyes pierced him with remorse. But there was nothing he could do to change things now. He felt guilty about having neglected them. At Christmas he sent a money order and a card from some faraway place, with a scribbled note of regret that he could not be with them. He wouldn't have come today if he had not realized that they would not be here much longer. It had taken some very smooth talking to persuade Mulligan and Harris to drive so far off their route.

"Larry always was very restless," Mrs. Hagen told Mulligan and Harris.

Mulligan smiled and winked at Larry. "Maybe we could talk him into settling down for a while."

"Time he had a family," Ben Hagen added.

"Your father's right, Larry," Mrs. Hagen chimed in. "You're no youngster now. Martha's three years younger than you and she has three children."

Larry shrugged. "I've always been too restless to put down permanent roots. The world's too big, too exciting. And there's so much of it I haven't seen yet."

Judith Hagen stood up suddenly. "You gentleman will think we have no manners. I'm sure you must be starving after that long drive."

"Don't trouble yourself," Mulligan protested. "We had lunch on the way."

"There's apple-and-blackberry pie fresh out of the oven," she coaxed.

"You've never tasted pie like Mom's," Larry told them.

He noticed Harris studying a collection of family photographs arranged on the table near the front window. The two little blond girls must be Martha's children that he had never met. There was one of his sister and her husband with the new baby. They had the settled, rooted look of people content to spend their lives in one place. He had always felt compelled to seek new horizons, craving the stimulation of contact with different people, driven by a restless urge to compete. Yet there was nothing in his world to which he was as firmly attached as to these two old people and the house in which he had been born. Attached by a tenuous thread of memories rather than actual physical contact. But it was something that he knew he could never make them understand, and his inability to communicate the special place they held in his thoughts created its own little ache of sadness.

Larry's mouth watered when his mother brought in a tray with wedges of pie and large scoops of vanilla ice cream softening against the warm pastry.

"Mmm...great pie," Harris complimented her.

"Worth making the trip just for this treat," Mulligan added.

Larry was disappointed with the pie; the pastry seemed tougher than he remembered from boyhood. Of course, he had come a long way and had eaten in many of the world's finest restaurants. He imagined the look of disbelief on his mother's face if he were to tell her that he enjoyed things like snails in garlic sauce, stuffed squid and other exotic dishes. They were plain folks and proud of it. He had heard her say it countless times in the past. But it was only now, that his own horizons were so expanded, that the statement had any real meaning for him. They were so much part of their placid environment that the places he told them about must seem like fantasies. When he spoke a few phrases in Spanish, French and Italian they were amazed and grew quiet.

Suddenly Larry realized what he had done. He had made them aware of how confined their lives had been, how restricted their horizons. The comparison with his own eager, restless life was forcing them to view theirs in a different perspective. They were confused and beginning to be gnawed by troublesome doubts. In their dimmed eyes he could see that they were thinking it was too late for them. Any moment now they might come to the bitter conclusion that life had passed them by.

"No matter where I've been," Larry told them in the assured, practical way that had convinced many skeptical people, "I haven't come across anything that beats this way of life. Believe me—there's a lot to be said for the things that don't change. And for the people, too." As their eyes brightened he knew that he had reassured them.

When Mulligan cleared his throat Larry glanced at the mantle clock that had belonged to his great-grandmother. It was time to go.

There were long, late-afternoon shadows on the lawn and dry, pale-yellow leaves whispered underfoot as they walked to the car. Larry embraced his mother, pretending not to see the tears on her wrinkled cheeks. Ben took Larry's hand in both of his and held it tightly. His lips smiled stiffly but his eyes were solemn and moist.

"Try to come back soon," he whispered. "We won't be here much longer."

Larry nodded, not able to trust his voice. Mulligan started the car and Harris opened the rear door, waiting for Larry to get in. The way Harris was standing with his arm propped on the door, Larry thought his father might notice the outline of the armpit holster. He quickly got into the car and Harris followed. They waved from the road and the old people waved back, then Mulligan accelerated.

Harris took the map from his briefcase and checked their route.

"I appreciate what you fellows did," Larry said. "It meant a lot to the old folks...I'll probably never see them again."

"You were smart to come back," Mulligan said.

Larry sighed and closed his eyes, shutting out the landmarks that stirred so many memories. What Mulligan and Harris didn't know was that someone had double-crossed him. Probably Deborah, to get even with him about Maria. A cablegram to the right people could set the wheels turning very quickly. Otherwise, how could they have known precisely where and when he would arrive? But he had played it cool when Mulligan and Harris closed in on him in the airport terminal. Instead of making a break, he had gone along quietly. It made more sense to tell them he had come back to face the music, even though most of the loot was gone now and not a chance of paying it back.

"There's a garage ahead," Harris told Mulligan. "Better fill her up."

As the car slowed, Larry felt a hand grip his right arm. He stiffened and opened his eyes. The handcuff clicked with the finality of a door closing him off from the world. The young detective sergeant had the other bracelet of cold, nickel-plated steel on his left wrist.

"You worried?" Larry asked.

Harris seemed to relax. "Not any more." He smiled slightly. "I've had a perfect day."

Larry closed his eyes and reflected that if he had any luck left at all, there would be no mention of his arrest for the mining stock affair in newspapers that might be read in the Riverdale area. What the old folks didn't know couldn't hurt them.

Eric Cameron's short stories, frequently broadcast on the air, are published in magazines and anthologies in Canada and the USA. His thoughtful, powerful story "Destroying Angel" appeared in our first issue, SSI No. 1.

"Yipin, I've never turned to you before,
but now I need your help."

A Wedding in Zhaojiatun

BY MA QIDE

BEFORE daybreak, like reverberating thunder, three firecrackers echoed suddenly over the village of Zhaojiatun. Mistaking it for an earthquake, the people around struggled into their trousers and rushed out into the street. Another three reports, followed by beating of drums, strings of small crackers and wind instruments persuaded them in the village that in fact someone was getting married.

It was quite true. Today was the wedding day of the son of Zhao Chengxiang, a newly rich villager.

By ten in the morning the courtyard was almost packed with guests, and Zhao Guangqi, the master of ceremonies, inquired of the host whether to declare the celebrations open with firecrackers and music.

"What's the rush?" said Zhao Chengxiang. "It's early yet." And he drew two Butterfly cigarettes from a new pack, gave one to

Zhao Guangqi, put the other between his lips and lit first the other and then his own.

"Chengxiang, for whom are you waiting?" asked his brother-in-law Liu Sanqing impatiently. "Can't you see the time?"

Since his father-in-law had passed away, Liu Sanqing had become a family "authority" whose word prevailed.

"Brother," Zhao Chengxiang hastened to explain deferentially, "my cousin Zhang Yipin, my eldest aunt's son, is coming today. Had you forgotten?"

"How could I? The one with the glasses that was paraded along the street with a black placard some years back and now works in the provincial capital?"

"Yipin is now deputy director of the provincial Institute of Agriculture," said Zhao with a smile, hearing the note of contempt for his cousin in Liu Sanqing's voice. "That's regimental rank! He insisted on coming to Guoping's wedding as soon as he heard. Say what you will, he's still got time for the likes of us, after all we're yokels and he's what he is."

Liu Sanqing blushed deeper than if he had been boxed on the ears but held his peace. Damn you, Zhao Chengxiang, he cursed inwardly, for the consummate toady you are! What you mean is, now he's a VIP with money, you're looking for a fridge or a TV from him.

As they were talking there came from way on the edge of the village the toot of a motorbike horn, which turned out to be that of Zhao Chengxiang's Suzuki steed that had gone to meet Zhang Yipin. And here was his son jumping off glumly, removing and slapping his snow-white gloves, taking his sunglasses from his nose and wiping them.

"What? Where is he?" Zhao Chengxiang asked his son in perplexity.

"Nowhere. He couldn't give a damn for us!"

"You've never met him, or maybe you took a wrong turn?"

"How could I have? I may not have met him, but I've seen his photo from when he went abroad. Tall, hair swept back, suit with a tie. Very elegant!"

"He doesn't drress like that all the time. Supposing he was

dressed casual? We're not all like you, with a Western suit on all year 'round."

"I'd know him dressed casual all right! The star attraction wouldn't come empty-handed, would he? Nothing grand, I grant you, but at least a thermos or a lamp or something, with "happiness" pasted on in red paper! And there was nobody like that, nobody I saw."

"Rubbish!" said the father with a glare. "He needn't bring a thing."

Guoping blushed and kept mum, feigning indifference.

"So what, then?" he muttered eventually.

"So what? Go back and get him!"

Just as he was turning the bike, Zhao Guangqi, the master of ceremonies, gave an abrupt cry.

"Uncle Chengxiang, it's himself now!"

Zhao Chengxiang craned 'round in astonishment.

"My dear cousin, why have you come on foot?"

The approaching guest was indeed his cousin Zhang Yipin, dressed simply in a white shirt, blue trousers and cloth shoes, the image of a county cadre on country business.

"I'm sure I must be late," Zhang Yipin apologized with a smile. "I hope you'll accept this small token of my appreciation." He opened his bag and took out a red satin quilt-cover of pure silk, which he had had someone buy in Shanghai the previous month and his wife had put aside rather than use. It was now being turned to account.

At the sight of it, Zhao Chengxiang's face went scarlet abruptly, though he chuckled on.

"Really you shouldn't have gone to all this expense for your own family. Well, if you insist. I'd hate to hurt your feelings."

Zhang Yipin's arrival had completed the score.

"Let the wedding ceremony begin!" called Zhao Guangqi at the top of his voice. In an instant, amid the deafening explosion of firecrackers and the shattering roar of blunderbusses, the musicians launched valiantly into a spirited rendering of *All Birds Court the Phoenix*.

"Second item—the reading of the guest list and the list of gifts!"

The music ceased forthwith and the noisy courtyard subsided into silence.

"Uncle on Mother's side Liu Sanqing, peasant, presenting one four-speaker Toshiba radio tape deck." The master of ceremonies sang this out then led the applause followed by the guests and jostling onlookers.

"Uncle by marriage on Mother's side Ma Qingbo, peasant, presenting one Sanyo twin-tub automatic washing machine."

"Uncle by marriage on Father's side Dong Lianqun, cadre, manager, Huaxia Industrial Company, presenting one Sharp 18-inch color television set."

The applause crescendoed, evidently owing to the magnificence of the gift.

Yet there was one of the guests who had begun to sweat, namely cousin Zhang Yipin, realizing his cousin's resentment of his paltry gift compared with this yard full of top-quality up-to-date furniture and electrical appliances. It had never occurred to him that others could manage to give such expensive things. Truth to tell, he himself could never have afforded a single one of them. To this day he had not changed his still treasured 12-inch black-and-white for a color set. Despite the assumption that he had returned from abroad with a selection of high-priced gadgetry, he had in fact brought back nothing more expensive in the way of gadgets than a single-speaker tape-recorder the size of a brick. His travel subsidy being very limited, he had bought it with money scrimped and saved by taking instant noodles and surreptitiously making them in his room.

Not that anyone would believe a word of it.

He regretted coming; he was sincerely busy at work and had an academic discussion to chair the next day. Staying away would have avoided this unpleasantness.

"People," his wife had said—and she was an upright and considerate woman in these matters—"have obligations. We must never forget cousin Chengxiang's kindness!"

He had thought about it and decided he had better come.

She was right. Where would he have been today without his cousin's help?

Twenty years ago today he was a starving schoolboy at the county town senior middle school with his eye on the district school-leaving and university entrance examinations, that key moment so fateful in life. "Those days," he was told, "decide whether you end up in straw sandals or leather shoes!"

The production brigade had long ceased catering, forcing the hungry schoolboy to turn for help to his cousin, then a cook in the county government canteen.

"Come here once a night," said his cousin Zhao Chengxiang softly, seeing him wasted away to an impossibly pitiful spectacle of great eyes and jutting cheekbones, "at nine."

Before a fortnight was up, the secret was out. One night Zhao Chengxiang was caught just as he was slipping some buns fresh from the kitchen steamer into his jacket. At the time, it was tantamount to stopping everyone else's gullet. He was criticized twice and dismissed and lugged his bedroll back to the commune.

Zhang Yipin regretted whenever he thought of it that his cousin had erred for him and him alone.

But he got over it eventually and passed the examination for the College of Agriculture in Beiping to boot. The day before he left he went to say good-bye to his cousin, who gave him a farewell dinner of elm-bark noodles. On the following day his cousin got up early, borrowed a wheelbarrow, lined it with straw, a mat and a clean mattress and said to him:

"Get in. I'll see you on your way."

Zhang Yipin wept, for his cousin's anger and ill health after his dismissal had left him a bag of bones and in no state to push a barrow.

"Look," said his cousin, hurt that he wouldn't get in, "if I could drive you there in a horse and cart I would. Just let me take you a step or two to say I did, will you?"

Weeping, he got in.

All that had happeneed twenty years ago.

Zhao Guangqi, the master of ceremonies, had come to Zhang Yipin's name:

"Uncle on Father's side Zhang Yipin, deputy director, provincial Institute of Agriculture—"

The blood rushed to Zhang Yipin's face at once. His head felt as if it would explode.

What came next was so bizarre as to make Zhang Yipin doubt his own ears, but the master of ceremonies announced:

"—presenting two 0.8 carat diamond rings and one West German camera!"

This in the ringing tones of an election result.

What was it all about? Zhang Yipin, temporarily muddled, looked up and darted a glance at the master of ceremonies, who responded with an ingratiating expression that said, "I'm sure you appreciate the kindness." He looked at his cousin who stood beside him with a broad smile, as though nothing were afoot.

As one who administers a bitter draught with his nose held, Zhang Yipin felt his innards heave ineffectually.

He shouldn't have come, really he shouldn't have.

The munificence of these occasions boils down to the drink.

Determined to put on a fine show, Zhao Chengxiang had laid ten tables instead of the usual, and acceptable, five or six, plus the best drink in the country instead of the local, and usual, Zhanggong, Bao-feng and Linhe, and not by the bottle but by the case, fifty bottles to the case and a cool twenty cases, which was quite a treat.

"This is my cousin," said Zhao Chengxiang by way of introduction when they had hardly sat down at the table to which he led him. "Yipin graduated from the College of Agriculture in Beijing with a diploma, which is worth more money than the worker-peasant-soldier things of a few years back. He was down on his luck, but he pulled through, and now he's deputy director of the provincial Institute of Agriculture. Last year he flew all 'round Canada and the States!"

This embarrassed Zhang Yipin. "Now, cousin," he said with a blush and a repeated wave of the hand, "there's no call for all of that, surely."

"Why, facts are facts. I mean every word of it," Zhao Chengxiang continued expansively. "I'm sure you all remember what put every family here in Zhaojiatun in the money last year: those new mushrooms. What you may not know is how those new mushrooms got from Japan to here. They didn't just come on the railways; they had to be *introduced,* otherwise they'd never have taken here in China, and it was my cousin's lot that did the *introduction!*"

The company's response was one of reverence for a comrade who, though unprepossessing, had put them, as a community, in the money.

"Well, I'll be blowed: you're a seed expert!"

"Tell me, Deputy Director, you wouldn't have any of that 820 multi-eared wheat at your place, would you? We're in bad need of the stuff, and we can't get it at any price."

"Quite right, Director Zhang. It would be a good turn. We don't need much. A thousand catties or so should do."

So will rural directness ask favors on first acquaintance.

"Well," said Zhang Yipin diffidently, "the 820 gave a bad crop last year. I can do you a bit, but I doubt if I can manage much."

"Now, now, we'll leave it for the time being, shall we?" Zhao Chengxiang chipped in abruptly to change the topic. "Let's get back to where we were. The drink may not be up to much, but I hope you'll do it the justice of having a few more. Come along now: fill your glasses!"

A non-drinker whose face reddened with a drop, Zhang Yipin took a symbolic sip and put down his glass.

"What's up?" shouted the sharp-eyed Liu Sanqing. "Here we all are, bumpkins compared with you. How'll we get on if you won't drink, eh?"

"Leave him alone, all of you!" said Zhao Chengxiang, extricating his cousin. "He's no head for it, as I know."

As he spoke, the bridegroom came up to do the honors with more drink, serving and toasting every guest at the table except Zhang Yipin. Silently, they turned in concert to look at the host Zhao Chengxiang, who didn't bat an eyelid.

No sooner had his son taken five steps away than Zhao Chengxiang surprised him by banging his fist on the table, shouting aloud to his receding son.

"You come back here, you bastard!" he barked.

The reprimand put Zhang Yipin in a spot.

"No matter at all!" he said, to smooth things over. "Really, I don't drink."

Lowering his head, the bridegroom went back resentfully to the leading table.

The thing with weddings is that however formal and mannerly they begin, they degenerate with drink into as bibulous and boisterous a free-for-all as at a public play.

Seeing that most of the guests had left their seats to get up finger-guessing games, Zhao Chengxiang clapped Zhang Yipin on the shoulder and addressed him conspiratorially.

"Yipin, I've never turned to you before, but now I need your help."

"Ask away. Anything that's in my power."

"It is, otherwise I wouldn't. This 820 of yours."

Thinking his cousin wanted strings pulled to buy the seed, Zhang was frank.

"I'll tell you straight, I shouldn't think I can get you more than a hundred catties or so."

"Take it easy, Yipin. I don't want to put you in an awkward situation. I've got the stuff, two thousand five hundred catties, not a seed less. I just need a small favor."

"What favor?"

Zhao Chengxiang glanced at the people 'round about.

"Write me," he murmured, "a certificate of quality saying the seed's from your institute."

"Where is it from?" asked Zhang Yipin guardedly.

"Qingxian County piggery."

Qingxian County piggery. That explained it. Last year's batch of the institute's 820, what with a rainy harvest and careless storage, had mouldered and had to be sold cheap to Qingxian as pig feed to ensure quality.

"I know the batch well. Bacterially infected and no good for seed any longer."

"So what?" chuckled Zhao Chengxiang, seeing his cousin was in the know. "It'll be sold out of the province through a layman, so what we say goes. Except you and me, no one in the wide world'll know. All you have to do is write the certificate." He stretched out one finger and waved it. "And five thousand yuan into the bargain! How about that? Hey? How many years' salary's that for you? You tell me!"

It had never occurred to Zhang Yipin that his cousin would ask him anything on this scale. He flushed all at once, at a loss what to say for the best.

Faced with his silence, Zhao Chengxiang let him off the hook.

"How about just considering it, Yipin? Bosses have difficulties of their own, I know, and this kind of thing isn't any one man's say-so. Well then, you think it over while I do the honors at the other tables. Got to fill up their hollow legs!"

It was not long before Zhao Chengxiang returned from his errand. He sat down again at Zhang Yipin's side and under cover of the finger-guessing game that Liu Sanqing and the others were playing in a single-minded assault on each other's sobriety, silently stuffed into Zhang Yipin's pocket a small red-paper package.

Flabbergasted, Zhang Yipin tried to fish it out and see what it was, but his cousin covered the pocket.

"Just a little something to tide you over, a round five hundred, the balance to await certification."

"Cousin, I couldn't possibly!"

"Ha, ha! There you go!" laughed Zhao Chengxiang, shaking his head like a rattle-drum. "How do I get through to you? It won't do, Yipin, not the way it used to for the likes of you, too honest for mud to stick. Tchah! Nobody believes in it any longer. It's no use. Rake it in and spend it: that's the knack. You may laugh, but isn't it?"

Zhang Yipin shook his head incessantly but said nothing.

"I know you're fainthearted. What is it, fear of losing that official hat on your head if you make a mistake? Am I right? It doesn't matter, I tell you. If anything crops up, on my head be it. How about that?"

"No. You misunderstand me."

"Then put me right. Are you afraid of me making too much money? It's not come in all that easily these past two years, you know. And the worry every hour of the day and night. I don't mind telling you the tax people stuck me with a fine. Three thousand I paid, and not a penny piece to show!"

So worked up did Zhao Chengxiang become as he spoke that the end of his speech came out in sobs.

Silence. Painful silence. A silence that gave away none of either's thoughts.

"Cousin," said Zhang Yipin suddenly, "I can't take this money." And he resolutely brought out the red package.

With extraordinary calm, Zhao Chengxiang took it and pocketed it.

"All right, Yipin," he said evenly, "I won't force it on you. Just let me ask you this: do you mind me going through with it?"

"Cousin, let me finish."

"All I want to hear is whether you mind that or not."

"I'll do anything else for you, cousin, but not this."

"Forget it. We'll drop the whole subject, shall we? If the answer's no, I'll be damned if I ever ask you again!"

Flying into a rage of shame that turned him lobster-colored to the roots of his ears, Zhao Chengxiang snatched up a bottle of "Lu's Old Still" liquor, tried to remove the top on the table corner, failed, angrily took his teeth to it and bit it open with a "ker-bung!" Taking two large tea bowls and throwing out the slops, he slugged them brim full of liquor, pushed one across to Zhang Yipin and raised the other himself.

"How's the drink, cousin? Answer me!"

"Fine," replied the other awkwardly. "It's fine."

"Is it poisoned? Answer me!"

"Come, come! It's fine, I tell you. No doubt about it."

"Well then, seeing as it's fine, and seeing as it's not poisoned, you'll damn well drink it!"

"Now, cousin, I...er, you've had a drop too much!"

"Too much on one cup? I'm not a kid to be kicked around like a football!" And he raised the bowl, drained it at a gulp, then flung it crashing twenty feet away with a guffaw.

"Zhang Yipin, I respect you. I do! I think I may say I've got to know you today." He gave a maniacal laugh, then his face suddenly fell, and he raised both hands and boxed his own ears, cursing the while.

"Zhao Chengxiang, what the hell are you sucking up to big shots like this for? Open your eyes and take a good look: what are you now, and what's he? Are you still stealing buns for him or sending him off to school in a wheelbarrow? You've no pride, Zhao Chengxiang! You're the lowest of the low!"

The bottle-warriors at every heady encounter on the field of befuddlement, wondering what Zhao Chengxiang's tears and curses were about, put down their drinks in succession and were soon gathered around.

"Oh dear, oh dear! Chengxiang's had too much!"

"Come on, help him to bed!"

"Guoping, get over here. Your dad's drunk!"

Supported by the sturdiest men, Zhao Chengxiang staggered indoors to bed, cursing and weeping all the way.

Zhang Yipin hurried on with all haste.

Less speed and he would miss the 105 train to the county town, and he still had much to do.

Tomorrow's academic discussion.

His key speech to the meeting.

Why couldn't he remember anything about the outline he had drafted, damn it?

The wedding had muddled his mind. What can you say? You have to go because it's family, and when you do go you end up offending your cousin!

He could have wept. Life was supposed to be easier when you were rich. And now they were, why was there so much less feeling in it than before?

Suddenly a blunderbuss boomed three times deafeningly in the distance, quite unmistakably in Zhaojiatun. The wedding was over, the gunners were instructed by the host to give his guests a parting salvo!

Tooting its horn, a Suzuki drove up pell-mell on the highway with Zhao Guoping in the saddle and Liu Sanqing on the pillion.

The lad was riding at full speed.

The bike screeched to a halt beside Zhang Yipin, and Liu Sanqing got off the back toting a bag.

"What's the rush?" he asked with a smile. "Is this bag yours?"

Zhang Yipin saw that it was indeed his. "Yes, it is," he said, embarrassed.

"Take it then, and be careful with it. It's got your camera and your diamond rings in it."

Zhang Yipin blushed to the ears.

The Suzuki roared off, swirling at speed back down the road with Zhao Guoping in the saddle and Liu Sanqing at his back.

Zhang Yipin stood rooted to the spot.

Subconsciously, he opened the bag and looked. Tucked inside was a piece of red material, the satin quilt-cover he had given Guoping.

Tears sprang to the deputy director's eyes. "Oh cousin," he murmured.

Ma Qide was born in 1944 in Tuocheng County in Henan Province. Soon after graduation from the People's University at China in 1968, he began his writing career. He is now a member of the Henan branch of the Association of Chinese Writers and editor-in-chief of the literary magazine Bailhuayuan. *This story was translated by Wen Xue.*

"I am the only offender, so I should be the victim."

Hunger

BY NAGUIB MAHFOUZ

IT was midnight and the luck of the cards had not once smiled upon the young and well-to-do Muhammad Abdel-Qawi. His losses increased and multiplied, coming to over forty pounds in less than three hours. This had been happening almost every night. Moreover, his bad luck no longer affected him. He went on playing, sipping his drink in a leisurely way and exchanging jokes with his friends. And as soon as he had left the green-topped table, he forgot everything that had happened.

However, on this evening he stopped playing as the result of an irresistible desire to go nowhere in particular but just to take a walk in order to breathe the fresh dewy air of early autumn. Excusing himself, he left his betting companions and strode rapidly out of the club.

The street was deserted, the weather pleasant and refreshing. A peaceful serenity calmed his overexcited nerves.

He walked with a light step, whistling softly though sometimes a little louder, taking a delight in strolling with no special object in view. After a while he branched off and took the road that leads towards Kasr el-Nil Bridge. He glanced along it as far as the other end and a sense of pleasure made him quicken his step. When he got to the beginning of the bridge, he slowed down the better to enjoy the cool night and his feeling so relaxed. At that late hour, only a few cars passed quickly by at long intervals. When he got a third of the way across, he saw a man in ragged clothes leaning on the parapet with his gaze fixed on the river. There was nothing unusual in this to attract his attention, and he continued on his way without giving the matter a thought. Having covered the whole length of the bridge, he slowly returned. The man was still in the same place and in the same position. He seemed to be half asleep, befuddled by the cool breeze. Suddenly Abdel-Qawi saw him straddle the parapet and lean over. Abdel-Qawi threw himself towards him just at the very last moment and seized him by the left arm before letting him fall onto the pavement. Emotion held him breathless. Attentively he scrutinized this man who was casting away his life, while the other eyed him coldly with drawn features. It was then that Abdel-Qawi noted his pale face and puny body.

"What were you going to do with yourself?" he asked.

He obtained no answer, and the man's expression remained unchanged.

What could drive a man to commit so beastly an act? he thought. Even an animal does not kill itself.

"Did you really want to kill yourself? Why? Let me smell your breath. Are you drunk, or mad? For goodness sake, speak, you animal!"

"I'm hungry," the man replied in a hollow voice.

"You're lying! Stray dogs find food, and I do not believe that a human being dies of hunger in this country. You must have some vice, drugs perhaps?"

"I don't blame you. You've never known what hunger is. Have you ever felt it? Have you ever gone to bed, one night after the other, twisting and turning with the pangs of hunger? And the cries of your children, have they ever pierced your ears because of their empty aching insides? Have you seen them chewing at straw, eating mud? Speak you who are a human being! And if you have nothing to say, how will you be able to understand and find an answer to this wretched problem of hunger?"

Indignant and skeptical, Abdel-Qawi asked: "Do you really have a wife and children?"

Offended, the man replied: "I was once able to maintain a home. I worked in the factories of Abdel-Qawi Shaker."

The young man jumped at hearing his father's name. On the point of losing his temper, he controlled himself enough to ask: "You were a workman, then?"

"Yes. I earned six piastres a day. I was loved and respected. I supplied all the needs of my wife, my mother and my six children. I was even more patient than the owner of the big factories, for I thought myself content with what I used to earn, whereas he was always complaining and finding ways to dock the wages of some and to pay others in driblets. It's true that my life wasn't comfortable or easy either, but I was full of hope for better times to come."

The man was silent. Happy memories seemed to have exhausted his strength and all his energy. Abdel-Qawi became impatient.

"Tell me, then, how did this sudden change come about?" he insisted. The man raised his right arm, or rather what remained inside the sleeve that hung from his ragged coat. Through one of the holes could be seen the end of a limb that looked like the foot of an old bench eaten away by time.

Pointing to it with his left hand, he said: "You see this? The machine fell on my arm and crushed the useful part of it. In one moment, from a skilled worker I became a useless object. After I was cured, humble, discouraged, I went to see my boss. He received me without the least pity, considered it to be my own fault and blamed it on my absence of mind. It was Fate, I told him. With a disapproving movement of the head, he gave me a small indemnity. I said that this tiny sum would soon be gone and that my family and I would die of hunger if he did not help us. He promised to grant me thirty piastres a month, and I was not able to get more. I then realized that my life was completely ruined, that my mother, my wife, my six children and myself were fated to be hungry and destitute. I found life hard, merciless. I drank it drop by drop. I exposed the stump of my arm to passers-by in the streets so as to arouse their pity to obtain alms. God knows what that gesture cost me! I accepted milliemes and hunted for crusts of bread in dustbins. The burden of my lost self-respect crushed me. I was consequently forced to sell the furniture of the room we lived in, even that which was indispensible, and for a ridiculous price. Our clothes wore out, my children are almost naked. Hunger ended by sapping the strength from our bodies. The complaints and tears of the little ones caused me my most atrocious suffering. Always to be hungry is for me easier than to see one of my children looking miserably at me, his eyes full of tears, and saying: 'Father, I'm hungry.' These torments choke me. I hate life, I hate the whole world, my helplessness eats my heart out. One of my begging companions said to me one day: 'You're like a delicate rich woman used to eating a pound of meat a day. You'll get used to this life. You'll harden your heart and you'll reply to your son when he complains of hunger in the same way as I do to mine, with a slap that will make him forget his empty stomach.'"

The man fell silent, worn out, helpless. The rich young man was getting impatient and looking for a solution to this problem that had so suddenly been placed before him.

"Is that the reason that led you to kill yourself?" he asked.

The man shook his head as if to say that there was yet more, and added:

"This evening, returning to that spot in the open air that we use as a place to live, I was astonished to find the children calmly sleeping. Had they then become so used to hunger that they no longer felt it? My wife and my mother were also asleep. I woke up the eldest of my children and drew him gently towards me. With his eyes scarcely open, he cried happily: 'We've eaten some hot bread.' 'From whom?' I asked. 'From Uncle Soliman, the baker,' was his reply. This name struck like a bullet right in my heart. My hand was clenched on his little arm, watching the change that came over his face as a result of the transformation in my own: 'This man, did he invite your mother to go to the bakery to fetch the bread, or did he come here himself?' And he replied: 'He sent it to us by his little boy.'

"Although nothing had confirmed my suspicions, I furiously pushed him away from me. My eyes rested on my wife's face. I was suffocating. Frightful visions began to dance before me. She was sleeping profoundly after having satisfied her hunger through that vile creature who loved her at one time and who is today trying to profit from this pitiful situation. And I understand...I understand with my principles that hunger has not destroyed and that are still alive in me, that are driving me to jealousy and anger and making me capable of committing a crime...Should I take the throat of that sleeping woman in my hands and strangle her? The criminal thoughts that invaded my mind nevertheless disappeared when my gaze fell on my children. What would they have left when they had lost their mother and then their father? I hesitated, I weakened. All the same, to calm my anger, I could not prevent myself from giving her a very hard kick before leaving. Her strident cries followed me. I turned towards the streets where I had become accustomed to beg and walked 'round aimlessly. My vengeful thoughts tormented me. Should I go back and kill the baker Soliman? Or rather lie in wait for Abdel-Qawi Bey and stab him? However, I am only a poor cripple. What can I do without my right hand? With all these feelings torturing me, my steps led me to this place. I saw the river. Its current hypnotized me, making me forget my sorrows, and I understood how I could put an end to this life. The Nile was really what I required. Destiny had led me here to show me the way to deliverance and repose. The idea of death little by little took hold of me to the point of dominating me completely as I thought of my infirmity, my weakness, my hunger, the complaints of my children and their sufferings. I thanked the good God for having been able to restrain my anger so as not to have killed my wife. By disappearing, I allow her to feed the little ones honestly, whether through Soliman or someone else it doesn't matter. I am the only offender, so I should be the victim. And when I was on the point of finishing it all, you put yourself between me and my deliverance. Do you understand now what a wrong you have done?"

The young man had listened attentively.

"Do you intend to do it again?" he asked.

"Without any question," was the calm and decided answer.

Abdel-Qawi smiled. He searched his pockets, found a ten piastre piece, and gave it to him, saying: "Take this. Tomorrow morning go to the factory where you used to work. I shall be there. Here is my card. Show it to anyone who tries to stop you coming in!"

He pushed the man well away from the parapet and added: "Put off your decision. There is still hope. I shall find you a job as a porter or no matter what. Let us go. You go home and be reasonable. But tell me, what is your name?"

Nonplussed, the man looked at him. He replied in a blank voice: "Ibrahim Hanafi."

Abdel-Qawi pushed him yet once more well back from the parapet, saying: "Do as I say, Ibrahim. Good-night!"

Thoughtfully Abdel-Qawi moved away. What chance was it that had directed his steps towards this place just at the propitious moment to prevent a crushing burden being placed on his father? In all simplicity, he thought that his walk and then his arrival at the decisive moment were certainly due to something much higher than chance or coincidence.

A thought suddenly passed through his mind that made him pucker his brows: How many families, in the same situation as Ibrahim's, could be made happy with the sum that I lose every night at the club?

Naguib Mahfouz, who was awarded the Nobel Prize for Literature in 1988, has long been recognized and honored for his literary output, especially in the Arab States. In 1970, Egypt bestowed upon him its National Prize for Letters, and the Collar of the Republic, the highest of its national honors. Maguib Mahfouz was born in 1912 in Al-Gamaliyah. He took his degree in Philosophy at Cairo University. He has also written for the theater and the cinema.

"He sat and brooded over the problem for many
  evenings at the local public house, much to
  his wife's annoyance."

First Prize to Miss Pettigrew

BY CAREY BLYTON

IT was time to plant the marrow seeds. At this time of the year Mr.
Peacock always felt the stirring of his blood, and the excitement of
the battle royal that had waged for ten years between himself and
Miss Pettigrew. Every year for ten years her marrow had carried off
the first prize at the local horticultural society's annual Fruit and
Vegetable Show, while he had had to content himself with second
prize.

Over the years he had tried his utmost to win the first prize, and
tried his utmost to discover the secret of Miss Pettigrew's giant
marrows. He had tried everything. They were both members of the
local horticultural society, and he had tried to pump her for
information at every opportunity: what sort of seeds she used, what
sort of manure, what sort of soil, how often she watered them. But
all inquiries Miss Pettigrew neatly side-stepped, with that slightly
vacuous beaming smile of hers. So he had resorted to subterfuge.

His wife accused him of obsession. Perhaps, over the years, it had grown to be such. He had taken to spying on Miss Pettigrew in an attempt to discover where she bought her seeds—there were several local nurserymen—but this had led to naught. He had even tried to trap her into giving him this information on one occasion. He had taken a packet of "Wellman's Gigantic" to one of the horticultural society's meetings and, during the break for refreshments, he had shown them to Miss Pettigrew and made extravagant claims for them.

"Now I know!" he had cried triumphantly in her face. "Now I know! *These* are the seeds you use!"

But, unfortunately, Miss Pettigrew had not denied this and then let slip the longed-for information. She had merely beamed at him in her vague sort of way and said:

"Oh, no, Mr. Peacock, I tried them once, many years ago, but I didn't think they were all they were cracked up to be."

Wretched woman! Mr. Peacock had ground his teeth and changed the subject rapidly.

This year, he made a really determined effort to discover what seeds Miss Pettigrew planted. He scoured the district, visiting all the nurserymen and seedsmen for miles around, asking discreet questions. He was really rather proud of his ploy. He thought it rather clever, in fact. Each and every one he visited he asked the same question in the same roundabout way:

"I'm sorry to bother you, but my sister...she's rather vague and absent-minded, you know...asked me to get her some marrow seeds. The trouble is, I rather think she's bought them already but forgotten all about it. So I thought I'd better ask before perhaps buying them a second time."

He then proceeded to describe Miss Pettigrew minutely, right down to the vague and vacuous smile. But he drew a blank everywhere.

Drat the woman! She obviously grew her marrows from each year's harvest, taking seeds from one to dry out for the following year. There was no way of finding out if this was so. But if it was—and Mr. Peacock felt quite sure of it after his vain inquiries around the district—then he would never be able to compete with Miss Pettigrew until he had one of her marrows. The thought had given him the idea.

One dark, early autumn night he had gone to Miss Pettigrew's garden, climbed over the bottom fence, and made purposefully for her greenhouse. He had made sure by discreet inquiries that she would be away, visiting her sister in Bournemouth. But a neighbor's dog, a rather large one, had taken it upon itself to visit Miss Pettigrew's garden for its own purposes that night and, when it saw Mr. Peacock creeping stealthily about, it had kicked up a fearful racket. So much so that the lights had gone on in Miss Pettigrew's next-door neighbor's house, and Mr. Peacock had had to beat a hasty retreat. He lost part of his trousers in the debacle.

By nature a law-abiding citizen, Mr. Peacock gave up thinking about Miss Pettigrew's greenhouse, and made no further forays into the enemy's camp.

This year, however, Mr. Peacock's obsession had become all-powerful. He was utterly determined to discover the secret of Miss Pettigrew's marrows, no matter at what cost. He sat and brooded over the problem for many evenings at the local public house, much to his wife's annoyance.

"It's really quite ridiculous, a grown man getting into such a state over a stupid marrow!" she said on more than one occasion.

His wife did not understand. It was a question of pride. Well, possibly male, chauvanist pride, "that a frail and silly woman should win the first prize, year after year, no matter what he did!"

He got the chance he was waiting for at the last meeting of the horticultural society. Miss Pettigrew was speaking to Colonel Fortescue-Blythe, and Mr. Peacock overheard her saying that she would be planting her marrow seeds on the Friday evening as she had to go to her sister in Bournemouth. Her sister was ill and needed looking after, and Miss Pettigrew was anxious to get the seeds in before she went.

Friday evening! Mr. Peacock found it difficult to conceal his delight, and he was even quite affable to Miss Pettigrew when she left the meeting. The wretched dog of Miss Pettigrew's neighbor had died that winter, so Mr. Peacock decided that *nothing* would stop him from finding out how Miss Pettigrew planted her seeds, and what seeds they were into the bargain. He could hardly wait until Friday evening came.

When it did so, it was a very dark one, with the gathering clouds of an imminent storm filling the sky as far as one could see in every direction. It suited Mr. Peacock very well indeed. "Dark nights for dark deeds," he chuckled to himself.

He told his wife he was going down to *The Fox and French Horn* and left the house excitedly. Now to find out at last! He approached the bottom fence of Miss Pettigrew's garden in a roundabout way, and was pleased to see that the light was on in her greenhouse. She was pottering about in it, as far as he could see from the shadowy figure glimpsed through the glass. He climbed the fence carefully, and came up to the greenhouse like a Sioux Indian approaching a White settlement, very slowly and keeping to all the shadows.

He reached the rain-water butt at one corner of the greenhouse and peered in through the grimy pane nearest to his hiding place. He had once commented unfavorably on the state of Miss Pettigrew's greenhouse glass, but she had murmured something about being able to afford a gardener no longer, and being too old and frail to clean them herself. Mr. Pettigrew was now glad of this, since he was able to look through the clear patches in the very dirty panes with less chance of being seen.

Miss Pettigrew was busy working by the light of a single 40-watt bulb, its faint light further reduced in power by grime and the visiting-cards of countless generations of flies. As Mr. Peacock had hoped, she was planting her marrow seeds, taking them from a tin box and, kneeling on a mat, planting them in a prepared bed that ran the whole length of one side of the greenhouse. She was talking to someone.

"We must win again, George, win again. That horrid Mr. Peacock must *never* win the first prize, must he?" Her voice was quite clear, and came through the hole made by a missing pane of glass quite close to Mr. Peacock's left ear. She suddenly chuckled, and Mr. Peacock felt the first raindrops of the storm hit his face. Thunder rolled distantly.

Who the devil was she talking to? Mr. Peacock was puzzled. The light was so dim in the greenhouse that he couldn't be at all sure if

63

Miss Pettigrew was talking to herself or to someone he couldn't quite see from his hiding place. She continued her planting and chattering.

"One more, George, and then we must go to bed. Got to be up early in the morning to go and see Muriel."

She patted the earth, and then rose. She left the greenhouse quite suddenly, and Mr. Peacock drew himself back into the shadows by the rain-water butt as she shut the greenhouse door and scuttled back along the path to the house. He heard the back door shut, and the bolts being pushed.

Mr. Peacock waited a few minutes, and then cautiously moved out of his hiding place and entered the greenhouse, closing the door very quietly. It smelled warm and dank. He switched on his torch and, carefully shielding its light, he explored. There was little to be seen. The marrow bed ran down one side of the greenhouse, and a workbench the other. He found the tin from which Miss Pettigrew had taken the seeds on the bench. There were still quite a large number of seeds in it. With suppressed excitement, Mr. Peacock took a good pinch of them and put them in his pocket. That would show the silly old biddy! Not this year, but wait until next!

There seemed to be no sign of any manure, natural or artificial. He shone the torch down onto the earth of the bed in which Miss Pettigrew had planted the seeds. He felt sure now that she used no manure or fertilizer, and a closer inspection would prove it. He knelt down, and very carefully sifted earth through his fingers, shining the torch close to it. His fingers suddenly met something in the earth, and he pulled it out into the light.

It was difficult to make out what it was, so he uncovered some more. He looked more closely, and then realized a lot of things with sudden clarity. George! Yes, he remembered now. He had been Miss Pettigrew's older brother, nursed by Miss Pettigrew for almost twenty years before it had become too much for her and he had had to go into a private nursing home. He had become senile, and kept wandering off. The last time he had wandered off and then vanished without a trace. All that had happened years before Mr. Peacock had moved with his wife to the village.

He looked again at the remains of the arm, still covered with mildewed and decayed clothing, that protruded from the marrow-bed. He really didn't have to look for any more. He knew. Poor old George. All these years he hadn't been pushing up daisies—he'd been pushing up Miss Pettigrew's prize marrows.

Carey Blyton has two careers: author and composer. He prefers the short story form and his stories appear in numerous publications; they have been broadcast by the BBC on local and national levels. As composer, he has written for the concert hall and recital room and also for television drama, television commercials and documentary films. He has combined his two talents in a number of spoof versions of such stories as "Sweeney Todd" and "Dracula" for schools.

"We're never going back, old man."

Summer of the Amphora

BY FRANCIS EBEJER

AUTUMN always filled him with a sadness for summer. But never like this autumn.

He looked out into the darkening street, watched the swirling dust and leaves from the smitten mimosas and oleanders, the last struggling vines, and thought of the long days of sun, the water of the bay, its Mediterranean shimmer, the young people.

When a splatter of rain flashed drops right up to the counter, he carefully removed a pile of newspapers and magazines from the edge, the rustle the paper made shocking him for awhile with images of stealthily enclosing waves.

It was rapidly getting dark. Outside, beyond the seawall and the sand, the sea was turning bronze with yellow darting flecks; the sky, too, was deepening swiftly; soon everything would be black, shut out. The street lights came on, but the small shop remained in darkness. He thought of lighting up but did nothing about it. He often stayed long in the dark these days, looking out to the vanishing sea. He did little but gaze out to sea, aware of the stealth of the enclosing waves.

"Old man...old man..." He could still hear their voices, watch their high glee. "Old man...an ice cream, a pair of flippers, a *granita,* a postcard, old man, a couple of sherbets, sun-oil, a paperback for a quiet read on the sand. Old man...old man..." They called right through the long summer days.

Then they were all gone, suddenly, with the first reaching-up of clouds whipped on by an autumnal breeze, the finally intimidated sun, the creeping chill in the air. The beach became deserted; the sea seemed to retreat within itself as it grew colder, hugging itself, a little grim now, its warm open invitation clamped shut.

One or two people, redolent of autumn evenings, came in for newspapers, a packet of envelopes, a magazine or two, tobacco, sweets, notepaper: people he had known all his life, grown old with, the permanents. They never mentioned the summer, as if for them, too, the evocation might prove too strong, too nostalgic to bear, and, for at least one person, himself, too heartbreakingly sad.

To think that only a few weeks ago it had been high summer. And she with the sweet, pensive face, the large, dark eyes, the young, healthy body; and the boy with her, not a year older, with the laughing serious eyes, the wild, sun-bleached hair...

They were both dark with the sun, holding hands, clasping and unclasping them. Together they had told him their story on that August afternoon, and he had half-listened amused and indulgently, his eyes on the brightly colored *luzzi,* each with the Osiris eye on its prow, out to sea on their way to the night's fishing.

They had bought two ices from him, then sat in their swimwear in the shade of his shop. For the first time, he had looked properly at the girl, and the shock of resemblance and memory had almost been too much for him. He had thought of amphoras.

Amphoras out of an ancient sunken Greek trader. And the biggest, most wonderful dive of his life.

So long ago. Fifty years? And *she* standing—exactly as this girl would, he knew it—on top of the highest rock around the bend from Delimara Point on the southeast coast of Malta where the sea was bluest with russet patches laced with turquoise and silver, silver especially, if, like them half a century ago, you happened to be there at eight o'clock on the morning of a summer's day.

He had long known about the amphoras, as he had known about her in the village, following her about with his eyes unconscious of the way his love was so evident. So, that day, there she was, olive-skinned and lissome, almost miraculously right on the spot where he had often daydreamed she would be one day to watch him dive for the old Greek oil jars.

He had dived from well over eighty feet, dived with a full pride in himself and a sense of immortality and limitless power. He had done it all for her, and, on resurfacing, had proudly held up the amphora for her to see. Even if not the largest, it was the most perfect of all, not a crack on it.

Tears dimmed his vision this August afternoon and, like an act of survival, he allowed himself for a moment to listen to this young couple's story. Breathlessly, all the time seriously, they told him the story of their love, the proud fathers in the village ten miles away, opposing them while feuding with each other from the doorways of their respective shops; their escape from home.

"You must go back, my children," he told them. "I should give up the whole idea. It isn't wise to run away. Later you may be sorry."

The girl shook her head. "They're looking for us. They won't find us and we're never going back."

She had an arm over her lover's shoulders and, for no reason that he could fathom, he almost felt as guilty as the obstinate fathers.

"I should give up the whole idea," he had said three weeks ago, surprised at the sudden hardness in his voice.

That other summer of fifty years ago, he had at last told the girl, after clambering up to where she stood motionless under the beating sun: "This amphora, it is for you." Her hand to her beautiful face, she had stood regarding him for awhile; then she had taken the amphora and hurried off.

He had changed quickly into his clothes and followed her back to the village, keeping several steps behind her and an eye open for the gossips.

Bunting and saints' statues and banners were up for the fiesta and a splutter of Chinese crackers smoked on top of a roof, the priest's. Women were placing geranium pots on their windowsills, calling out cheerfully to one another as they did so. A couple of dogs had chased each other across the village square, bandstand in place, and round and round the village water pump just as the church clock struck tinnily above him. Unforgettable day.

Only once had she looked back, then hastened her steps, clasping the amphora to her with both arms, her long, slim skirt raising lingering seconds of dust tendrils.

For a whole week after the fiesta, he did not see her. During the fiesta itself she had stayed with the other girls of the village. Each time that he had passed near the group, in his best clothes and with a sprig of mint wedged dandily behind his left ear, she had lowered her eyes or else turned away to speak to her companions.

Then after a week of waiting, he saw her again coming out of church. He waited until she had turned into a narrow deserted street before overtaking her. All he could whisper was: "The amphora?" She had said: "In my room." Joy filled him.

A month later, unwilling to wait any longer, he had gone to her father. Both her father and mother had liked him immediately. Then he went again and again, until, on the seventh occasion, her father called her into the warm kitchen where they were sitting, and told her how much they liked him, how much they desired him as a son, and what a good husband he was going to be to her. He had been very lucky there: her parents liked him.

"You must go back," he told these two young people several times all through the hot afternoon, barely four weeks ago—yet a past eternally recurring.

Fifty years ago is now; it *is* once more. Exactly the same, with a little difference here and a little difference there. *Her* parents had liked him; yet, the custom being such then, he couldn't be with her. *Their* parents had declared war; yet, thank God, they could still be together. And yet, this was also foolish; they must go back, seek peace that would rebound on their future, surely.

"Old man...old man..." He left them for a moment to sell three ice creams, then returned to where they were sprawled on the sand, their beautiful, serious faces close together. "Go back, listen to me, go back."

She had never put her arm around him, let alone her face to his: that was also one of the little differences.

He had never married. The moment of the amphora and the girl he had loved so much had been the only brilliant time of his life.

And then one evening, while he was downstairs with her father, mother, brothers and his own parents, they heard a crash in the room above them, and he knew instantly what it was.

She had come down tearful. "I'll get you another one," was the first thing he had said, bravely, loudly, hiding his disappointment.

He had never got her another amphora, never dived again in his whole life. And when, in later years, he thought of the remaining amphoras beneath the blue water, he was only sad.

She had stopped weeping and was looking at him. In the clamor of her family and his, anxious for his sake, for well they had known how he had prized the amphora, he desperately wanted to understand her caged look. What was she trying to tell him?

At last, "I understand," he had said, truly understanding everything.

"It slipped from my hands," was all the explanation she had given.

"I understand."

This August afternoon had dwindled to a little light on the horizon. There were still a few bathers though. He broke into the couple's silence. Determined to ease the situation, he patted the boy on the knee, saying lightly: "Now come on, you two. Up you get. One last swim and back home you go. It might cool your hot heads down a bit."

He was surprised at his own levity, even more surprised when they obediently and wordlessly stood up and, with arms around each other's waist, went off like gold-streaked waifs into the water rapidly turning to bright copper.

He watched them from the shop. The day's shouting was done; the last bathers—no more than three far off along the beach—were rubbing themselves dry. The sun's final reflection had turned blood-red all of a sudden beyond Delimara Point with the strange rock formation of an immense sad-eyed mother holding a child on her lap.

He heard the girl calling, both already chest-deep in water: "We're never going back, old man."

He waved to them, smiling indulgently to himself. "Ah, their mischievous ways," he mused.

The sand, the sea, the sky, the young people. He thought about the perfection of the day, even with all his regretful recollections and these young people's problems. He smiled again and waved as, once more, the girl's cry reached him: "We're never going back, old man."

A brief swirl of wind tossed more dust and sand into the shop. The bay was now completely black, not a glimpse of star above it, and a fresh wind rising. The *luzzi* would be hard put to sail at all tonight. The young wind moaned in impotent imitation of its bigger brothers of winter.

And with the wind, the ghosts of all the summer sounds and sights, the voices, the shouting, the calling, the singing and the laughing seemed to invade his little shop, whirl unstoppably around him. Through it all, there still came to him the one truly distinct voice, calling out, the one he would always hear and recognize till the last moment of his life:

"Never going back, old man."

First, the strong swimming out of the two; then, her lifted arm as she called out for the last time from the first of the enclosing waves. Forever unfolding with that last cry inside his brain, would be his own voice suggesting the last swim of that enchanted day—his tragic interference.

Now as fifty years ago. With a little difference here, a little difference there.

Yes, he had understood only too well the message of her look that day when the amphora broke; the agony she must have gone through trying to comply with ageless custom and her parents' wishes; the desperation of the moments separating her from the one she had truly loved. And it had not been him.

Beautiful, spirited girl; ahead of her time?

Differences?

Inside the storage vaults of his memory, there echoed to this day, even after fifty years, the crash of the amphora—at last her own personal gesture of refusal, of defiant self assertion.

Like a lifted arm glimpsed for a moment and then completely gone, far out to sea, last summer.

Born and raised in Malta, Francis Ebejer is a successful short story writer, novelist and playwright whose work appears in Malta, England and the USA. His early plays are credited with starting the modern theater in Malta. A bilingual writer (English and Maltese) he also writes and produces television plays.

"He had been unable to shrug off the persistent thought that his eyes had not deceived him in the dusk..."

Tuatara

BY CECILIA DABROWSKA

THE sooty shearwaters had come back to the coast and islands of New Zealand by November when their returning migration flight from the North Pacific was ended. Upon the rocky northern end of the harbor entrance they clustered in a colony and made their burrows in the sandy soil, and laid the single white egg that both parent birds would incubate. Daily at dusk the shearwaters came in toward land in silent flight to relieve their mate on the nest, calling to the other as they landed at the burrow entrance.

The man seated on a rock in the half light watched the gliding flight of graceful avian silhouettes, black against the pale western sky. Beyond him the cliffs rose sheer to the skyline and against the fading light on the cliff top the twisted limbs of the *pohutukawa* trees stirred in the wind. In a month they would be flowering, bearing the crimson blossom that earned them the title of Christmas tree in New Zealand.

Motionless, Peter Vincent stayed there, unmoving enough to be part of the rock; loosing as he relaxed the burden of work, tasting the small untimed rebellion against time's too rapid passing. His gaze lingered upon the birds, the sea and the cliffs, inspecting the scene minutely as an artist might, not letting his love for it blunt his perceptions.

Between the rocks and the cliffs, stunted mountain flax and small patches of scrub grew in a profusion of mingled greenery. The birds continued to land, filling the dusk with raucous cries to their mates.

And then in the thinning light Vincent found himself staring at a rock shape, sculptured as though a lizard form straddled the crest of it. Puzzled, he leaned forward a little, not taking his eyes from the lifelike silhouette. Dimly he could trace the lifted saurian head, and faintly distinguish the serrations of a crest running along the length of the body and tail. In the deceptive light he thought he saw it move, and accounted the movement a visual distortion. Landing shearwaters filled the space, and when he looked again the silhouette was gone.

Idly puzzled still, the man looked at all the rocks once more and could find none crowned with a saurian profile. He stood up to leave the beach, and as he turned he looked thoughtfully out to sea, at the broken topped darkness of Karowa, a host island of the tuatara reptile.

The same puzzlement brought Vincent back to the lonely shore in full daylight three days later, and again he sat exactly as before and studied the rock shapes. There were none which could have been misconstrued, even in darkness, into dragon semblance. He shrugged off the improbable thought that had lingered in his mind, and looked away at the sea and bird life.

He contented himself with watching those things, yet finding a vague dissatisfaction with the sea birds, as though the scene offered something more that remained hidden from him. Lingeringly he left them, intending to leave behind also his own half-formed belief in what he had glimpsed in the dusk.

Looking down the beach, the cliff tops reared like a battlement, turreted with the stark iron strength of the *pohutukawa* trunks.

Vincent wondered how long ago these trees had lain in a crevice in the rock as thin obscure brown threads—nothing more—and taken root in the soil there. In the long years they had thrust down, widening the fissures, sealing themselves to the cliff top, trailing binding roots down the outer face of the high place.

Annually blossom crowned their tormented grotesquery of spray-beaten limb, and leaped like wild fire in the sea winds. He glanced up as he walked, seeing the plump roundness of furred buds among dark leaves, and the grim aerial roots clinging to the multiple holds of the cliff face, exposed to the battering winds.

Again dissatisfied, he left the shore.

Peter Vincent came back once more, and this time he walked along the cliff top overlooking the sheerwater colony and the rocks where he usually sat. From this high vantage point he watched the scrub and nesting ground below. He had been unable to shrug off the persistent thought that his eyes had not deceived him in the dusk, and that what he had seen for a flickering moment had been a living reptile.

An hour went past and still he waited, held there in that lonely place by a hunter's patience, baffled curiosity and something very close to certainty.

Twice he was on the point of leaving, of consigning the whole idea to the winds, and disregarding it with finality; but he settled back again, occasionally looking out to sea, or down upon the foaming curve of the inrushing tide. Another hour slid away, the sun reached towards early afternoon.

And then, startled, his eyes marked a space among the coastal vegetation, a little to his left, far down below.

Lying there on the cliff top, Vincent saw the dark, trailing reptile shape cross the open sandy soil, and without haste make its way out onto a rock, and settle there in the sunlight.

Slowly his tensed body relaxed, though he did not take his eyes from the reptile. All his vague suppositions were turned into reality—the motionless tuatara was clearly visible. A thousand conjectures rushed through his mind—incredulity still struggled against visual proof. He continued to stare downwards, not quite able to believe the obvious substantiation of all queries, grappling with an affirmative answer when he had been taught automatic negative; unwilling almost to accept the living proof because it had appeared there like a small incomprehensible miracle.

Grasping at actuality, the watching man was struck anew by the thought that the tuatara might be only one of a colony, or that, extraordinarily, it might already have lived alone through a century of solitary survival. And if no such reptiles had lived in a wild state upon the mainland since white settlement, could it possibly be one which had been brought from the coastal island many years ago, and escaped upon the mainland? Or even be the offspring of such a captive one—for solitary reptiles have produced young after considerable seclusion from their mates.

The careless owner of such an escaped one would shrug off the loss indifferently, and thus ensure that subsequent reference to it contained little interest and accounted it long ago dead.

Had anyone else ever known of the tuatara's presence? Did others once see the reptile, and seeing it not recognize it, or knowing, discount it utterly? Who had once lived in the locality? What things had these people known and relinquished with fading memory?

Vincent's mind circled the problems of the tuatara's survival. How would it find sufficient to eat when not hibernating? Did it drink from rainwater pools in the hollows of the rocks, when occasional rain fell? He knew that on this deserted and unfrequented strip of coast the reptile was unlikely to be molested by stray dogs. The fact that it had adjusted to its present environment was indisputable; and that environment had few factors similar to the natural island habitat of other tuataras.

There were the shearwaters with which it shared a burrow, and there were the scattered flax bushes and scrub which would harbor insects and small lizards for food. Perhaps it ate the young of the shearwaters also.

Knowing that he had already spent too much time away from work, Vincent dragged his mind back from the fascination of conjecture and stood up to leave.

The tuatara still sat there unmoving far below him, as though it were carved of stone or was a petrified survivor of the mists of creation.

He walked back along the cliff top the way he had come.

Step for step with the man, as he went about the task of running a lonely coastal farm single-handed, the image of the tuatara kept pace—lingering uppermost in his mind, superseding all other distractions.

Vincent wanted to see the reptile from much less distance than previously. He knew that the sense of territoriality in most living creatures would confine it to inhabiting one burrow, and probably to sunning itself daily on one particular rock near the burrow entrance.

Accordingly, two days later when time permitted, he went back to the shore and entered the belt of scrub in the locality of the rock where the tuatuara had previously basked in the sun. Cautiously as a trespasser he moved past the shearwater burrows that riddled the soft earth, and settled himself among the mesh of branches to wait. This time there was a sense of expectancy and certainty—the sure knowledge that the reptile would appear.

The wait seemed a long one and Vincent did not see from which burrow the tuatara emerged, but his eye caught the first sign of movement as it approached the rock.

There in the hot somnolence of the shore scrub it came crawling, with only the small rustle of fallen leaves pressed beneath its slow moving feet to give a whisper of its coming. The underside of the reptile's body and tail touched the soft earth as it moved. The beak-faced head was lifted, watchful and alert, oval eyes wide staring. Upon its skin the yellow spots gave back gold for gold where the intruding sunlight touched upon its trailing length. The prominent spines on its body formed a serrated crest from the back of its head to the end of its tail. Through the mellowed light of the bushes it moved soundlessly, traveling with slow primeval pace.

Unhurriedly it emerged from the leafy overhang and made its lingering way across the loose sandy earth, pausing on the exposed aridity of the rock, settling itself there. Judging from the very prominent crest and the long, large build of the reptile, Vincent decided it must be a male of the species.

Absolute protection shielded these creatures from harm, and

their survival only upon the coastal islands of New Zealand guaranteed their freedom from lawless interference. The tuataras themselves were cloaked in the mystique of being a "living fossil"—akin to the fossil dinosaurs—a treasure remote from public gaze, guarded in natural isolation. Generations had seen them only inside the terraria of aquariums and zoos.

And yet here the man had witnessed the slow crawling gait, the beak-faced stare, the timeless ancient unhaste—out of all believable habitat—taking place incredibly in a mainland nesting ground of the shearwaters. The tuatara, splay-legged on the rock, moved its head a minute fraction, and he found he had been holding his breath momentarily, astonished.

Vincent looked away from it, questioning that this was truly its natural habitat, knowing that it must be, for tuataras brought over to the mainland were given the planned passage of kings, and had likewise no escape.

He watched fascinated by the reptile's completely motionless stance, for the tuatara was the possessor of time. The blurring of weeks, months and years would make no impression upon it; and ultimately the passing of a full century would be met with the same indifferent blank stare, the same slow-paced ageless survival. It stared into the shadows—the drifting fall of leaves—feeling the warmth of an ancient sun, watching down the century.

Time seemed weaponless against the antiquity of these creatures' lineal descent, unbroken from the Mesozoic age; for they had lived contemporaneously with the dinosaurs, and become one of the most outstanding unchanged living conquerors of unthinkable epochs, that left the present century floating like a mote in the dust of all eternity. Their present remote island habitat and guarded welfare had left them with progeny assured into countless tomorrows.

In an hour the tuatara made no further movement. The nagging realization of time passing and work waiting, turned the watching man's thoughts from it. Cautiously he detached himself from the net of branches and turned, reluctant to go. Once he looked back still in wonderment, but the reptile was there, the motionless clear-cut Triassic profile unmistakable in the hot sunlight.

Vincent told no one what he had seen. Ridicule would await him, and if he did share the knowledge, what sort of fate awaited the tuatara? A small stab of possessive jealously cautioned him into reticence as to its whereabouts. With wry amusement he recalled the Maori protestation that the *taniwha,* the mythical water dragon, could no longer be seen, because the white man's weapons of ridicule and disbelief had driven it into hiding. Conversely, had constant denial of the tuatara's presence led likewise to rejection of any possible extraordinary mainland survival?

But he knew that all the carefully gathered facts of these creatures' island existence pointed to such a survival being utterly impossible. Diametrically opposed though mythology and actuality might be, the line of truth in the Maori utterance counseled his actions now.

Disbelief and ridicule, Vincent mused, would leave him emptier than if he had never spoken, for they dispossess a man of his treasure and wither his dreams. Once afraid to dream, he becomes cowed enough to retract out of misplaced human respect, despite the knowledge in his heart, or when his eyes have beheld impossible things.

And so he told no one, but whenever he looked toward the cliffs and the shore it was as though he and they were bound together in conspiracy.

It was three weeks before Vincent again saw the tuatara, though he had gone twice to the shearwater colony to look for it, and had not time enough to spare for a protracted visit.

Snatching time from work's burden to devote it to something that was truly time's possessor, he did not wait in vain.

Placing himself where he could see several of the burrows, he sat watching. It was early afternoon and the summer sun poured warmth onto the sand. There was a slight movement at a burrow mouth, and as he watched the tuatara's beaky upper jaw and jowl showed in the sunlight, then the paler serrations on its neck, followed by its small forefeet, protruded from the hole. The creature paused there basking in the sunlight, making no move to emerge farther.

It held Vincent there where he was, as though its presence was irresistible. He leaned slightly forward, peering through the mask of branches, studying the crested head and all that was visible of the reptile's forepart.

Looking down upon the olive-colored body with its ridges and folds of skin, he could see no sign of the pineal or third eye in the center of its head, for it must long ago have been covered by scales, though it would once have been visible many years ago when the reptile was a hatchling.

Vincent knew that the third eye was not believed to be connected with vision, nor to be sensitive to varying degrees of light, nor to have any heliothermal purpose. The third eye existed in some reptiles long before flying reptiles or bird life appeared on earth; and the conjecture that the median eye was a defense against such airborne creatures has been discarded, while no definite proof has been found that the eye acts as a thermo-receptor. Its purpose remains inexplicable.

He knew also that it is by the bones of the skull and abdomen that the tuatara is separated from the true lizard order, and this necessitated its being reclassified many years ago, as a member of the *rhynchocephalia*—the beak-headed reptiles. The combination of skeletal differences places the tuatara apart from all recent reptiles. Fossil remains of the Triassic beak-heads found in the northern hemisphere showed remarkable similarity to the present-day tuatara.

Watching its motionless saurian profile Vincent's mind sought beyond it, attempting to identify the reptile with incomprehensible time spans. In a wide swing, imagination by-passed all mankind's history, all known and unknown civilizations, counting down the ages of the earth—dismissing Quaternary, Tertiary, pausing at the Mesozoic—balked finally by unaccustomed reference from evaluating even that as it truly was.

His mind tried to grasp the whole of the fantastic picture, attempting to see it complete and comprehensible, as measured somehow in simple perspective against the world of today. He thought of the Mesozoic dinosaur, iguanodon, then deliberately magnified it many times over until it stirred in his mind's eye, reared in full Triassic omnipotence. He met the staggering thought of titanic thews moving heaving flanks in the terrible pangs of endless appetite to support gigantic life.

Vincent wondered if the long ago ancestor of the tuatara, though a contemporary of other dinosaurs, had principally inhabited another part of the earth. For what then had saved the small tuatara, of a length rarely exceeding twenty-four inches, and possessing a low metabolic rate, from the ravages of later reptiles—the flesh-eating tyrant dinosaurs—in the following ages of evolution? Any original enlarged size would have availed it nothing against such as they.

Had continental drift, or colder climate helped isolate the species in safety in an area where the larger dinosaurs were unknown, or had perished early of climatic change? Two hundred million years of evolution had caused the disappearance of the beak-headed reptiles from all parts of the earth but one—the coastal islands of New Zealand, where the tuatara, the sole surviving species of that order of life, continued to increase.

And still the man pondered in wonderment as to how this one came to be where it was. Had it once cut its way from out of the swollen leathery egg, forcing through the shell, and burrowing upwards through the loose soil, to find itself freed in a habitat far harsher than nature ordinarily confined the species to? Could such offspring have truly survived here, coping with adverse conditions? Would an adult tuatara, escaped and forgotten, brought here before strict government protection was enforced, adapt itself to the mainland where once they had lived?

And when the early settlers reached New Zealand, where had they found the specimens that undeniably were on the mainland? Were the reptiles living in a wild state? Or had the Maoris acquired them from coastal islands and fed them to keep them alive? It seemed highly improbable that such was the case, for the old Maoris felt great revulsion for the tuatara and all lizards.

Even as he watched, the sunlight vanished behind cloud, and the tuatara was robbed of its warmth. The rising wind, cold from the sea, ruffled through the bushes. There was no flicker of change in its posture—it seemed indifferent to the altered temperature of its surroundings. Half an hour later it sat there, unmoving, unblinking. Reluctantly the man withdrew, watching to see if the slight movement of the branches about him attracted the reptile's attention. The tuatara remained where it was, motionless and undisturbed.

It had been dusk when Vincent had first glimpsed the reptile, a month before, while it was on its nightly hunt for food. Twice he had missed seeing it at night, and determined curiosity drew him back. In the fading light he waited near the burrow mouth. All about him the landing shearwaters plummeted down, their loud cries filled the night air, though they paid him little attention. The returning bird inhabiting the burrow which the tuatara shared, landed at the entrance and started calling. First to emerge from the burrow was its mate, which joined it with answering cries.

In the creeping darkness Vincent's eyes almost deceived him. The tuatara emerged from the burrow entrance—a dark primordial shape—timeless æons in its slow reptilian crawl. For a while it stayed there not far from his motionless presence. He saw the lively curve of its limbs, as though it sat with elbows crooked. There was in its posture the confirmation of innate wariness, a tautness of the crested head, as though it could and would change rapidly from seeming indifference to anger if provoked.

He was surprised by the speed with which it moved toward the bushes, traveling rapidly as a lizard—the trailing trunk and tail lifted from the ground. Alert and hungry, it was hunting.

Faintly through the darkness he saw it pause awhile to sight its moving food, then dart its head down to seize the beetle. A few moments later it disappeared among the bushes.

He went away, treading carefully between the shearwater burrows in the midst of their caterwauling, leaving the tuatara to its night hunt.

Six weeks after Vincent had discovered the tuatara the storm came.

On the coast where there was always wind, the rising pressure was not at first noticeable. By nine o'clock at night the gusts had strengthened savagely, and one hour later the wind was roaring toward storm velocity.

Far up on the cliff top the *pohutukawa* trees moaned in the fierce wind, their branches grated one against the other in the enormous sway of distorted limbs—wind-dragged toward the land. The pull of limb against anchored trunk strained the trees backward, so that they thrummed with tension and quivered against the leash of the rock face.

The force of the exposed roots clinging all down the outside of the cliff exerted monstrous pressure as those in the crevices refused to yield their hold, yet strained incessantly backward from it.

The tap roots jerked back and forth in the rock fissures like iron snakes—the tension relayed downward into the rock until it too failed to absorb any more. Behind the roots the rock face opened—a great split ran along the cliff top. The trees now leaned into the wind toward the sea.

Precipitated into imbalance the *pohutukawas* reeled from the cliff top in a high aerial confusion of stricken limb and wind-torn blossom. Their branches flailed in a frenzy, wide flung, lashing as though to stay themselves on those of their fellows. They plummeted downward, destroyed by their own arboreal habit.

With them came the rock fall. Hundreds of tons leaned away from the cliffs, broke into great pieces and dropped, smashing on impact into a hurtling cascade that smothered the nesting ground below. Behind them came other falls.

Vincent had woken in the night disturbed by the wind's fury. And finally above the sound of the storm he had listened to that other menacing sound rise and slowly abate. He knew when he heard the great falling thunder of the rock face that the wind had reaped the *pohutukawas;* and the tormented trees ablaze with seasonal fire had plunged from the cliff and taken with them hundreds of tons of rock that would obliterate everything in its path.

In the first light he went down to the beach, filled with consternation and foreboding. The shearwater colony, as he had known it, was destroyed. Familiar outlines of rock shapes were gone. Beneath the great sprawling mounds were the tuatara's rock and its home burrow. A pang of despair gripped him as he climbed across the piles of gray granite.

He had welcomed the tuatara's presence as others welcome good fortune, or the benevolence of fate—it had come to him like sudden wealth, with the gift of its presence sufficient.

The great cliffs had become a cairn on the empty beach, holding his secret entombed for all time. Harsh death spread beneath them—crying gulls drifted far above them. Shredded *pohutukawa* flowers, wind-driven, extinguished the bright fire of their blossom in the cool crests of the sea.

There amidst the rock fall Peter Vincent paused, knowing the tuatara was dead.

He turned his back upon the huge monument of the storm and he told no one.

Cecilia Dabrowska grew up on a farm in the Manawatu district, where she acquired a deep love of animals and great respect for the forces of nature. For awhile she taught school but left to marry a Polish emigré, now a citizen of New Zealand. Mrs. Dabrowska's work combines uncanny insight with skilled craftsmanship. Her stories are published in New Zealand, Great Britain and the USA. Her story "Huntress" appeared in SSI No. 62.

"Everything is loaded against me."

Crunch Point

BY RODERICK WILKINSON

HENRY Collitz walked in the autumn sunshine through the university courtyard with his raincoat over his arm and a slim briefcase under his other arm. He was a man about forty, tall, black-haired and it was his tight-set mouth more than his liquid dark eyes that reminded you of many people you had seen from places inside Europe. He was an intense man.

Collitz lectured at the university on business administration. He was a good lecturer—terse, sharp and lucid—and he had the reputation for reducing bigheaded managers to their proper size from the lectern when he was conducting a session. He had a cutting tongue and suffered fools rarely. His specialty was "The Reality of Management," on which he had written books and articles for years. *Harvard Review of Business* had quoted his material many times and his fee for in-plant training sessions was expensive.

Now he was losing his wife. He had the sense to see this months ago when Ed Chambers joined the university faculty from Cornell and he turned out to be an old friend of Connie's. There is every difference in the world between an old friend and an old sweetheart, and only a blind man could have missed seeing the difference that night when the three of them dined together in the restaurant in Chicago. Chambers was still single, Connie was still beautiful and Henry was feeling something he had never experienced before in all his life—jealousy. Connie and Ed Chambers were picking up something in the garden of their younger lives that was enshrouding them in eye-misting happiness. She couldn't hide it. Chambers couldn't. A whole world of talk and glances and laughter was being woven around these two, a world Collitz didn't know or couldn't grasp.

Nobody was trying to hurt anybody. It was just happening under their noses. Collitz knew their lives were changing. The only insurmountable handicaps that he could not change. He knew it before the blow fell at all. He dreaded the news when it did come because nobody in his life had ever told him before that there could be a possibility of one half of his life being destroyed, leaving him with the half he could not tolerate for a second.

He loved Connie. She was nearly ten years younger than Henry and it was as simple and as complicated as that. If he had loved only part of her—her figure or flaxen hair, for instance—it might have been different. She had her husband's love of *all* of her—her mind, her personality, her talk, her walk. She returned only part of it. How small a part this was never crossed her mind until that day she met Ed Chambers again after all the years apart. Then she knew that the part she gave her husband was ephemeral.

Somehow he knew it, too. Like a man under death sentence, afraid to ask the executioner for the precise date and time, Henry lived, ate, worked, slept under the same roof as his young wife knowing that the end was near. And he knew that living without her was not possible.

It took him quite a long time to start hating Chambers, surprisingly long for a man with such ferocity of feeling. At first he blamed it all on himself; this did not last long because the man who lectured on "The Reality of Management" was a rationalist. And common sense told him that he had done nothing to sterilize their marriage. Then he blamed Connie for a time. Although he could see and feel the struggle she was putting up to save herself and Ed from the cauldron of their love, he mentally demanded more of her.

As he walked through the archway to the carpark he remembered with agony how, inevitably, it had all come out the previous evening before dinner. It was their wedding anniversary.

Connie was lighting the candles at the table. She was wearing a royal blue dress and her blonde hair took on the sheen of the low lights. Her face was pale. She put the spent match in an ashtray and looked across the table at her husband. "Henry."

His black eyes glowed and his whole body stiffened, waiting. "Yes?"

"It's no good."

There. It was out. He even felt the warm glow of relief as he walked slowly to the sideboard. "Connie—don't say any more."

She was staring at the gleaming silver on the table. "It's no good, Henry. No, no good at all."

He poured drinks. "We'll move to Pennsylvania."

She said nothing.

He brought the drinks over. "Connie, I love you."

She remained staring at the table.

He set her drink beside her. "Tomorrow. We'll move right out to Pennsylvania University. No explanations. No good-byes. Nothing. They've been wanting me there for months to teach management subjects."

She looked at him and her eyes were glistening. "You don't understand, Henry, do you?"

"Yes, I think I do, honey. I think I do. Everything is loaded against me. We have no children. You knew Ed out east years ago. He's unmarried. He's your own age. I've been away too often lecturing. You've been seeing him. It's a fever—"

"Henry, it is *not* a fever."

"It's a fever, honey! Give it time. And distance. And reality." He knew as he used the last word that it was a mistake.

She spoke softly, pityingly. "Reality?"

The storm broke. He banged his glass on the table. "Yes—reality, Connie. You're married to *me*. You're not married to Ed Chambers. He doesn't have a wife. All *he* has is a degree in Chemical Engineering. I have a wife—you. And *that's* the reality of this crazy situation. You are *my* wife."

She was crying. "Henry, I *love* him."

"You *can't*. You're infatuated with him, and he with you. You've hypnotized yourself into this romance."

"Oh, stop psychoanalyzing me. You don't understand. I'll die without him. I *love* him."

His voice was low. "How can you say that? You married me. And I say I'll die without you." His eyes were glowing. "Connie, this is a sickness—"

"It is *not* a sickness, Henry." Her face was pale and cold as she faced him. "I want a divorce."

His hands were gripping the tablecloth tightly. His knuckles were white as he crouched, head bowed.

"Henry!" Her voice had a sob. "I want a divorce. Ed wants to marry me."

A strangled cry of savage rage came from his lips as he heaved the tablecloth and lurched back, holding it in his hands. "NO!"

The crash of dishes, silverware, glasses, food and cutlery was deafening as they exploded over the room.

Now it was today. Now he was walking over to the carpark where Connie sat in their open-top Vulcan. He could see her gleaming blonde hair and the red of her woolen jacket. She smiled bleakly as he opened the car door and got in. She switched on the ignition. "Did you have a good day?"

He threw his raincoat and briefcase over the back seat. "I was lecturing all day. As usual."

"I thought we'd talk." She steered the car towards the university exit gate.

"I thought we'd talked it all out, Connie."

They said nothing as she drove them down State Street. The sky was ice-blue and there was the first faint feel of an autumn wind come up from the lake. The shafts of brilliant sunshine beamed between the grand shadows of the tall buildings, gleaming on the thousands of cars.

Connie said, "Let's go up the Prudential Building."

"Okay."

She turned the car towards Grant Park. "We'll be able to see for miles on a day like this."

He put his arm along the back of the seat and turned to look at her beautiful face sadly. "D'you remember the last time we went up on that tower?"

"Yes, I think so." Her voice was small.

"We'd only been married a month."

She parked the car and they walked through the echoing vastness of the marbled vestibule towards the row of elevators. One was signed, "Express to Observation Tower." They went in with four other people. The elevator sighed its swift climb up forty-three flights to the azure sky.

All the vast geometry of Chicagoland was below them as they looked down through the double-glazed windows. Sun-drenched buildings stretched for miles along the lakeside; ribbons of streets, roads and railway tracks snaked into nowhere. And the ant-like cars crawled in thousands through the labyrinth of the big city.

Behind them was the rooftop restaurant, low-lit and modern in its sheer luxurious decor. As they watched the city's crawling millions below there was a voice just at their shoulders. "Hello, Henry. Connie." Collitz turned round quickly. The man who spoke was short-statured, bulky, well-dressed and he held out his hand.

"Hello, Walter," said Collitz, shaking hands. "What brings you—" He stopped and his face hardened in anger as he looked at the lawyer.

Connie said, "Henry, can't we sit down in the restaurant?"

Walter Heburn looked a little ill at ease. "Sure. Let me buy you a drink."

Collitz looked at Connie then at Heburn. "Who asked you—?"

"I did, Henry." Connie touched his arm. "Please let's talk, with Walter."

"Talk about what?" Now his eyes were gleaming with fury. "You never give up, do you?" He raised his voice. "When I need a lawyer, I'll send for one, Heburn. And you can bet it won't be you any more." He turned towards the exit then looked at his wife. "You conniving witch!"

He left them.

***

Through the echoing corridors and empty halls of the university his footsteps click-clacked as he walked down to Conference Room 80. Ed Chambers frowned as he passed the darkened, empty classrooms.

He opened the door of the Conference Room. It was a room set out semi-circularly with seats and desks. Although there were switch-on lights at every place, none of them was lit, and the room was in darkness except for the floodlit podium and small stage. The large, sweep-round blackboard, the rolled-up cinema screen, the tape recorder, the flip-chart and the felt-board were all illuminated sharply in the bright lighting. The auditorium and the desks were in darkness.

Henry stood behind the podium. He said, "Come in, Ed."

Ed slowly walked into the room and closed the door.

Henry said, "Will you take a seat, please."

Ed slowly sat down near the middle of the room and said, "What's the idea, Henry?" He looked puzzled.

Collitz came forward to stand beside the podium and leaned one arm casually along its edge. "I'd like an hour of your attention, Ed."

"What for?"

"I promise I won't waste your time."

"I thought you asked me here to talk tonight. About Connie and me."

"That's right. I did, Ed. And that's what I intend. What I'm asking is that you let me talk first—for an hour."

"Just you?"

"Just me. Then, I promise, I'll be quiet or I'll answer any questions you put to me or join any discussion you want. Will you give me an hour?"

"Okay." Ed sighed and crossed his legs.

Henry softly and slowly walked to and fro across the brightly-lit stage. He said, "You and I are here tonight because we have a problem—rather we have three problems. I am in danger of losing my wife. You want my wife. My wife wants me to divorce her." He turned and wrote these things rapidly on the blackboard, then continued: "Now, love is a matter of emotion. It is *not* a matter of logic. No cybernetic device or biological analysis has ever been developed which can explain to a man or a woman why they happen to love or should love each other. It would be useless, therefore, if I made any attempt to reason a way out of *any* of these problems. All I can say is that I love Connie; I have always loved her and she is the only woman I have ever needed or wanted. That is how I *feel*. But what I am going to try to do tonight, by the production of certain facts, is save my marriage, keep my wife and therefore save myself from a fate, as the old-time dramatists said, worse than death. And I mean that, *every word*."

From that point onward, Henry gave the most professional lecture of his life. He used the flip-chart to show exactly in dollars and cents the monthly standard of living to which Connie had become accustomed and he showed her outstanding debt. He used the felt-board to show estimated examples of Ed's salary and bachelor expenses. He rapidly drew up a balance sheet on the blackboard and reasoned the figuring to show the hard economic facts of Connie living with Ed. Then he moved to the blackboard and as he wrote occasional headlines, said, "The real problem about living with a woman, Ed, is that there's no textbook to tell you what it'll be like in advance because every woman's different and most men are liars. What I am now giving you is privileged information. My wife, the woman I love, sleeps till ten every morning, never darns socks, can't cook anything except by frying, has an expensive mania for handbags and hats, plays bridge atrociously and has dandruff which is difficult to detect. In our years of married life she has taken to her bed for at least four weeks every year with one of these illnesses: laryngitis, gastro-enteritis, migraine, fibrositis, shingles, chickenpox, a broken ankle, slipped disc and influenza." He held up a heavy file of papers. "And here is all the documentary proof of what I say; morning calls at ten charged on my telephone account every day for years, bills for new socks, her unsuccessful enrollment in evening cookery classes, bridge scores, bills from downtown stores for hats and handbags, and doctors' prescriptions for the ailments."

The lights went out. Henry pressed a button on the podium. The screen rolled down automatically and was illuminated by a projector switched on at the rear of the room. Henry said, "Let me show you some color slides of parts of our domestic life. These are the ones we always remove before showing slides to our friends at home."

He flicked the handswitch and there was a picture of Connie frowning shrewishly and looking like a woman of sixty as she looked into a shop window. "This one caught Connie off guard one Saturday morning at our supermarket." There were dozens of other pictures: Connie with her hair in curlers, Connie a little drunk at the Meburns' New Year party, Connie asleep in the sunshine with her mouth open, Connie grinning foolishly as she waved good-bye to someone at a bus station, Connie in a swimsuit. "Did you know she is slightly bow-legged?

"Now let me show you something you haven't even dreamed existed, Ed: Connie's family. I'll bet you never thought she *had* one. First, Connie's mother." Henry showed a slide of a thin, middle-aged woman with a pale, dry face. "You'll have her to take care of within a year," he said. Then there were slides of the cousin who was a struck-off doctor in Ohio and her gap-toothed young brother. "It wouldn't surprise me if he never makes High School," Henry commented. There were slides of her dead father who "began retiring at thirty-five" and her older sister who "insults all your friends when she meets them." There were two aunts. "You'd better send them money regularly; they've been broke all their lives," Henry said. Then he showed slides of an old uncle who was a lush and turns up once a month drunk, and of an older brother who has to be financially bolstered occasionally because of gambling.

The lights went up. Ed's face was drawn and pale. He said, "Everybody has problems. What're you trying to prove, Henry?"

Collitz pointed at him, his eyes blazing. "I'm going to prove to you that you *have* to love a woman like Connie to live with her. Sure, Connie has problems. For example, she snores. She has hiccups after a glass of lemonade. She can't stand the smell of coffee. She sweats more than most other people. Sure, she has problems, Ed, but I'm going to show that *you* can't live with them for the rest of your life. You don't have the emotional resources. Now watch this movie. I took it at a lakeside summer camp two years ago. It shows Connie trying to fish for pike."

The lights went out. Henry talked on and on, describing that vacation at Muirville.

When the room was lit again Ed had gone. His seat was vacant, the door was closing gently and Henry could faintly hear his footsteps fading down the corridor.

Quietly, almost sadly, he picked up a duster, erased his notes from the blackboard. Then he turned down the flip-chart pages, removed the felt-board signs and went behind the podium, leaned on it heavily with his elbows, his shoulders hunched. He stood there a long time.

The light click-clack sounds of a woman's heels grew louder from out in the corridor. The door opened and Connie stood looking at him. Her eyes were red. She said, with a sob in her throat, "What—happened to Ed? He—passed me downstairs. Wouldn't look at me."

Henry looked at her from his hunched position and said quietly, "Ed? I think he found what he was worth, Connie."

She leaned on the nearest desk, staring. "What—did you tell him? What did you talk about?"

Henry straightened up and said, "Connie, I told him what I want to tell you now. I married you because I loved you. I love you now dearer than ever before. To me, you're my princess, my dream-girl come true, the only woman in my life for the rest of my natural days on this earth, in sickness and in health, in richness and in poverty—" his voice dropped "—till death do us part. I love you, forever and ever." He stopped. "That's what I told him."

She sat down slowly, slumping, her shoulders heaving as she sobbed. Henry came·over to her, put his arm about her and said tenderly, "Let's go home, dear."

They went out together.

Roderick Wilkinson is a Scottish writer, broadcaster and lecturer whose stories, books, articles and plays have been published and broadcast in many countries. His short stories currently appear in magazines in the U.K., U.S.A., Belgium, Holland, Germany, France, and others.

"They like us as people to laugh with,
  not to suffer with."

A Point of Identity

BY ES'KIA MPHAHLELE

IT was not until a crisis broke upon Karel Almeida that I began to
wonder how he had come to live with us in Corner B location,
seven miles out of Pretoria. It was first rumored that he must be
well-to-do. Then people said he *was* rich. And then people went
around saying that he had won a huge bet at the race course
wherever (no one cared to know where exactly) it was he had come
from. Soon it was said that he was a colored African. And then
again they said, *ag,* he's not "colored," just one of these blacks
with funny names. All these guesses arose from the fact that Karel
Almeida was light in complexion, large in physique, and had
improved the appearance of his three-room house within two
months or so of his arrival. Also, Almeida laughed a lot, like "a
man who had little to worry him." But I shouldn't forget to add that
he was a bachelor when he arrived, and must have been saving up
and living light.

This was little less than ten years ago—I mean when he came to
our street and occupied a house next door to mine.

During those years Karel Almeida became "Karel" to me and my
wife and "Uncle Karel" or "Uncle Kale" to the children. We were
very fond of each other, Karel and I. We had got to take each
other for granted, so it was normal for him, when he was spending

his two weeks' leave at home and my wife fell ill, to look after her and cook for her and give her medicines while I was away at school, teaching. He worked in a Jew's motor-mechanic shop in the city, and lived austerely enough.

Karel's whole physical being seemed to be made of laughter. When he was going to laugh, he shook and quivered as if to "warm up" for a take-off and then the laugh was released like a volley from deep down his large tummy, virtually bullying the listener to join in the "feast."

"Hm, just hear how Karel is eating laughter!" my wife would say when the sound issued from Karel's house.

"Me my mudder was African, my farder was Portugalese," Karel often said in conversation. "Not, mind you, de Portugalese what come an' have a damn good time an' den dey vamoose off to Lourenco Marques. But de old man went to LM an' he got sick." After a pause he burst out, "An' he die sudden, man, just like you blow a candle out, T." He always called me "T" which was an intimate way of referring to me as a schoolteacher.

"Where were you and your mother?"

"In Jo'burg, man. It's now—let me see—one, two, three, ja, three years. Died in Sibasa, man, way up nort' Transvaal. My Ma nearly died same day and followed my Pa de day he die. Fainted an' gave us hell to bring her back. She went to LM for de funeral."

"And now, where's she?"

"Who, my mudder? She's dead—let me see—one, two, two years now. I brought her wit' me to Jo'burg when I was learning mechanics at de same garage what brought me here. Good Jew boss, very good. He got a son at university in Jo'burg. Nice boy too. My ma didn't like Jo'burg not dis much, so I took her back to Sibasa."

We often teased each other, Karel and I, he was so full of laughter.

"I can't understand," I said one day, "why you cycle to work and back instead of taking a bus. Just look how the rain beats on you and the wind almost freezes you in winter." He laughed.

"Trouble wit' you kaffirs is you's spoiled."

"And you Boesmans and Hotnotte are tough, you'll tell me."

"An' de Coolies, too. See how dey walk from house to house

selling small t'ings. Dey's like donkeys, man. Can't catch dem coolies, man. You and me will never catch dem. It's *dey* who'll always make de money while we Hotnotte an kaffirs sleep or loaf about or stick a knife or plug a bullet into someone or jes' work for what we eat an' live in an' laugh at life. Jeeslike man, dey's gone dose Coolies, dey'll beat us at makin' money all de time."

"But Hotnotte, Boesmans and Kaffirs and Coolies are all frying in the same pan, boy, and we're going to sink or swim together, you watch."

"OK. Kaffir, let's swim."

"What you got, Boesman?"

"Whisky, gin and lime. But you know, I'm not a Hottentot or a Bushman, I've got Euro*pean* blood straight from de balls no zigzag business about it." And, as he served the drinks, his laughter rang pure and clear and solid.

"But serious now, true's God, I've always lived wit' Africans an' never felt watchimball, er, discomfortable or ashamed." He could never say "what you call it." "Damn it all man, if my farder slept wit' mudder an' dey made me dat's dey business. You, T, your great-great-great-grandmudder may have been white or brown woman herself. How can you be sure of anyt'ing? How can any Indian be sure he's hundred percent India? I respec' a man what respec' me no matter his color."

He spoke with vehemence and compassion.

Karel took an African woman to live with him as his wife. She was a lovely woman whose background was unknown. She was hardworking and Karel treated her with great affection. She never had much to say, but she was not proud, only shy.

And the crisis came.

If the whole thing did not begin to set members of a family against one another or individual persons against their communities or vice versa; if it did not drive certain people to the brink of madness and to suicide; if it did not embarrass very dark-skinned people to sit in front of a white tribunal and have to claim "mixed parentage," then we should have thought that someone had deliberately gone out of his way to have fun in creating it. The white people who governed the country had long been worried about the large numbers of colored Africans who were fair enough to want to play white, and of Africans who were fair enough to want to try for "colored." They had long been worried about the prospect of one coffee-colored race which would shame what they called "white civilization" and the "purity" of their European blood. So, maybe, after a sleepless night someone ate his breakfast, read his morning newspapers in between bites, walked about his suburban garden, told his black "boy" to finish cleaning his car, kissed his wife and children goodbye ("don't expect me for supper, dear"), went to the House of Assembly and began to propel a huge legislative measure through the various formal stages to the President's desk where it would be signed as law. Whatever happened, a board was established to re-classify colored Africans to decide whether they were to remain on the register as "coloreds" or "natives." All people who said that they were "colored" had to go to the board for "tests."

They were ordered to produce evidence to prove their ancestry. (Was there a white man or woman in the family tree or not?) The onus was clearly on the subject of the inquiry to prove that he was "colored." Day after day papers were filed: birth certificates; photographs; men, women and children came and lined up before the board. A comb was put into their hair; if it fell out, they must have straight or curly hair and so one condition was fulfilled.

"How tall was your father?" a board member might ask.

"This high," an exhibit might reply. If he indicated the height by stretching out his arm in a horizontal direction, it was likely that the exhibit was "colored;" for Africans generally indicate height by bending the arm at the elbow so that the forearm points in a vertical direction. Another condition fulfilled or found to be an obstruction.

A family woke up one morning wondering if they had been through a dream: some of its members had been declared "colored" and others "native." But how was it possible that a whole family could experience the same dream? Once a "native," one had to carry a pass to permit one to live in an area, to enter another, to look for work in a town. It would be an indefensible criminal offense if one failed to show the pass to a policeman. Once a "native," one's wages had to be lowered.

"Look, man, T," Karel said to us one cold evening after taking a seat in our kitchen. "I must go to that board of bastards."

He took us by surprise. He took a cup of tea from my wife and stirred it in exaggerated circular movements of his whole arm from the shoulder. He might have been paddling a canoe, with that arm that looked like a heavy club. The tea slopped over into the saucer.

"To the board? But you don't have to tell them you are a native African?"

Karel looked down.

"What de hell, no." I looked at my wife, and she looked at me.

"I told you my farder was Portugalese. Dat makes me 'colored,' nê?"

"I know, but..." I did not know what I wanted to say.

"Look man, T, I—I can't go dress up in de watchimball, er, pass office dere for dis t'ing what you folks carry. Listen, T, I see youse folks get stopped by de bloody police day an' night: I see you folks when de whites at de post office want you to show your pass before dey give you a parcel or watchimball, er, registered letter; I see you folks in a line-up on Sunday morning when police pick you up for not havin' a pass in your pocket an' dey take you to de station. Look man, T, one night you don't come home at de time your wife's waiting to see you, eh? Now she gets frightened, she t'inks, oh, my man may be locked up. She look for de pass in de house and dere it is you forgot it. She puts on her shawl an' she takes de kids next door as she locks up de house an' she goes to de police station. Which one? Dere's too many. She t'inks, I must go to de hospital? Maybe you's hurt or knocked down. But she's sure it must be some police station. No one wants to ring de different stations to fin' out. Hell man, she's lost. De papers tell us all dis plenty times. Sometimes it's de last time she saw you in de morning when you goes to work. Maybe you couldn't pay your watchimball, er, admission of guilt and de police sentences you. Dere's a lorry waiting to pick up guys like you wit' no money for admission or who t'ink you'll talk for yourself in de magistrate court. A white man takes you to his farm far away from here to work like slaves. Maybe you die dere and your wife will never see your grave. T, never-never."

I was struck dumb. What argument could one have against this recital of things one knew so well? Hadn't one read these accounts in the press? Hadn't one seen and known personally families who had waited for a husband, a son, a cousin, who was never going to come? Hadn't one read these accounts in the press and felt something claw inside one's insides and creep up to the throat and descend to the lower regions until one seemed untouchably hot all over?

I ventured to say feebly. "You wouldn't be the only one, Karel. Isn't one strengthened by the fact that one is not suffering alone?"

"I ain't no coward, T. What about de wages? My wages will go down if I simply agree I'm black. Anudder 'colored' man may push me out of dis job."

"But you *are* African, Karel. You as good as said so yourself often. You came to live with us blacks because you felt purity of blood was just lunatic nonsense, didn't you?"

"Look man, T, de word 'native' doesn't simply mean one's got black blood or African blood. It's a p'litical word, man. You's a native because you carry a pass, you can't go to watchimball, er, Parliament. You can't vote, you live in dis location. One can be proud of being an African but not a *native*."

"What does your woman say about this, Karel?"

"Oh, you know she never says not'ing to dis'point me, T."

"But do you know what she thinks?"

"Can't say, T. Sometime she seems to say, Yes, sometime No, but she always say, Do what you think is the right thing, Karel."

My wife and I were sitting up one Saturday night when she said, "Why does the man keep talking about this like someone who cannot hold hot roasted pumpkin pips in his mouth? Why not go and get the paper to show that he has 'colored' paint on him instead of ringing bells everywhere to tell us he wants to go!"

"No, no, Pulane, you're not being fair. As far we know, he talks to us only about it."

"*To us only, ugh!* You should hear people talk about it in the whole street."

I did not try to ascertain if she meant the whole street, but said instead, "I think he wants to be sure first he will be doing the right thing."

"Ag, he's just a coward, finished. Just like all 'coloreds.' Blacks are nice and good as long as a 'colored' man is not told to become black."

"Why should anyone want to be black?"

"Isn't it that he wants to show the white people he's 'colored'? Isn't it that he thinks we blacks are nice to live with as long as he doesn't carry a pass as we do and get the same wages as we do? See them. Paul Kruger told them they were like white people and were civilized. Now you go round this corner, 'colored' people have better houses; you turn round that corner, 'colored' people get better money; you go the bioscope, the 'colored' people sit at the back and we blacks are put right in front where we can almost kiss the, er, what's its name? *Ag,* they make me feel hot between the thighs, these 'coloreds'!"

"Would you not want these good things they're getting?"

"Of course! What kind of question is that?"

"But you are not asking to be a 'colored' woman are you?"

"*Sies,* me? Would you like to see me 'colored'?"

"See what I mean! And you seem to want Karel to carry our burdens as a price for liking us and living with us. Who are we to say the 'coloreds' should not want to keep the good things they have?"

"I just don't want people having it both ways, that's what. They like us as people to laugh with, not to suffer with. We are the laughing, cheerful blacks, the ones full of life and entertainment, the ones they run to when they're tired of being 'coloreds,' Europeans, Indians. As for the Indians, they like their curry and rice and *roti* and money and mosques and temples too much to pretend they want us for next-door neighbors. I can't blame them because they don't try to bluff anyone. Look how the Indian boys run about with 'colored' girls! They want nothing more than to keep their business sites and help us shout from the platform. *Ag,* they all make me sick, these pinks."

She stood up and took the kettle from the stove with the force it would require if it were glued on. She filled it with water and put it back on the stove, all but throwing it down.

"And you think the Indian folk who join us in protesting are merely bluffing? And the whites, the Indians and 'coloreds' whose homes smell of police uniforms because of unending raids, and who are banned and sent to prison—are they just having a good time, just putting on a performance? Well, I don't know, child of my mother-in-law, but that is a very expensive performance and not so funny."

These had been times when I wasn't sure myself if I didn't really feel as my wife did.

After a spell of silence she got up to make tea. Meantime I went out to stand on the stoep. For some strange reason, while I looked at the blazing red sky over Iscor steel works five miles away, I thought of Karel's wife. The gentle-looking nurse who never said much any time...

Back inside the house, my wife said: "I wonder how much longer it is going to be for us Africans to keep making allowances and to give way to the next man to turn things round in our head, to do the explaining and to think of others' comfort."

I looked into my cup, looking for something clever to say in reply. I could not find it, But I know it had something to do with the African revolution...

"I got de identity card at last," Karel said casually a few months later.

"So!"

"De white trash! Dey wantin' to trap a guy all-a-time, bastards. Man, T, *hulle dink altyd hulle hol 'n mens toe*—dey t'ink dey goin' to drive me into a dead corner, sons of white bitches." He paused. "Been waiting for papers from LM. My late Ma put dem in a box and sent it to LM." He looked tired and uninterested in his achievement. His voice and posture spelled humiliation to an embarrassing degree—or was it my own embarrassment? Perhaps. I didn't have the courage to ask him to give the details of the examination which must have dragged on for a number of days with a number of breaks.

"So you'll have to leave our location and the law's going to pull you away from your wife."

"I been t'inking about dat, T. Dey can do all dey want dey'll never do buggerall to me and my woman, true's God. An' I don't take back my identity card. I stay 'colored' and live wit' my woman."

I thought about my wife's talk about people wanting to have it both ways.

Nor did Karel make any effort to leave Corner B. But we knew that the location's white superintendent would sooner or later be sticking a rough twig between Karel's buttocks to drive him out of the location.

Meantime, Karel's right leg had begun to give him trouble. He was complaining of sleepless nights because of it. He tried to maintain an even tempo in his life, and his laugh was still loud, clear and full. Even so, in the ear of one who knew him as well as I did, it was losing its roundness and developing sharp edges. When the autumn rains came down he complained more and more. He could not pretend any longer that he did not need to limp. He visited the General Hospital times without number. He was subjected to radiography countless times. The doctors prescribed one thing after another—to drink, to massage.

"*Ag* man, T, dese white doctors are playing around wit' me now. I do everyt'in' dey tell me an' al dey do is shake de blerry head wit' sandy brains. Dey loudmout' when dey tell us dey clever educated but dey know f-all. *What can I do,* man, I ask dem. Dey'll kill me wit' dat X-ray one day."

I felt by proxy the leaping fire that must have been scorching its way through him to release the tongue of flame that spoke these words.

One night Karel's wife came to wake me up to come to him. He wanted to see me, she said. I found him on top of his blankets, his face wet with perspiration. His wife was still fully dressed, applying a hot fomentation.

"Have you ever heard of such a miracle!" his wife said. Before I could reply she said, "Karel is talking in parables, I am sure, *hau!* He's telling me he wants to see a witch doctor. *Hei,* people, *Modisana!*" She looked at him as she was taking out tablets from a bottle. "Just ask him."

"Listen man, T, I'm told some of dese watchimball, er, witch doctor guys can do it. If de white man is beaten maybe black medicine will do it, man."

"Now you're not going to do such a stupid thing," his wife said. I had never heard her speak with such authority, such a bold face. Here on the question of sickness and patients, I felt, she was sure of herself. Looking at me: "I would rather take him to another hospital far out of Pretoria, borrow money somewhere, spend all my savings to pay white doctors. Tell him, you're his friend, tell him, maybe he'll listen to you." She stooped to give him his tablets. He turned and lay on his back, with a deep round sigh.

"Listen, T, my woman here t'inks maybe I don' show t'anks for her goodness to me, for her watchimball, er, patience, for her good heart. Hang it man, T, I'm grateful from the bottom of my heart, dat's jes' why I want to make it possible for her to rest a bit. She works too hard and has to sit up de whole night a'most lookin' after me."

"What should a woman be for if she is not there to look after her man?" asked his wife.

"But—but a witch doctor, man, Karel!" I said.

"You see him as he is," his wife said. "His boss has given him a month to stay home—on full pay you hear me? If he rests his leg for a while maybe we'll see which way we are moving. Maybe I can get a few days off to take him out to my people in the Free State. Just go away from here a bit."

"I think you should do what this good woman advises, Karel. Forget this witch doctor madness. Besides, soon as these chaps start mucking around with one's body they're sure to meddle with parts they know nothing about."

"That is what I keep telling him, you hear."

I was less convinced about what I was saying than I may have sounded. There were always stories about someone or other who had been cured by a witch doctor or herbalist after white doctors had failed. The performers of these wonders—as they sounded to be—were invariably said to have come from Vendaland in the farthest recesses of the rain-making queen's territory of the Northern Transvaal. Some time before this a school principal in Corner B had asked a herbalist next to his house to give him a purgative. He had almost immediately become ill and died on his way to the hospital. The herbalist had been arrested, but had pleaded that he had advised the teacher to take plenty of water with and after the herb, which thing he must have failed to do. No one had seen him take the herb who could say whether he had followed the instructions or not. Most of us, whether teachers or not, whether townspeople of long standing or not, believed one way or another in ancestral spirits. The same people might at the same time tolerate the Christian faith, or even think their belief in ancestral spirits reinforced by it. How could anyone be sure? A man like Karel trying to ride a huge wave of pain: what use was there trying to tell him not to seek help outside the hospital? What he said to me the next moment was disarming.

"Listen, T." He paused as if he had forgotten what he was going to say. "Listen, de doctor at de hospital says to me yesterday, he says I'm sure you got kaffir poison. Kaffir poison, you mean what dey call native poison? I ask. He says, Yes. I say, You can't take out kaffir poison? An' he says, No, he says, it's not for white medicine. An' again I says, What do you t'ink doctor? An' he shows me he doesn't know."

"And you think he was telling you what to do without saying so?"

"Yes, dat's not funny. You see for yourself how dese whites queue up at de African watchimball, er, herbalist's place at Selborne."

"Those are poor whites," his wife hastened to remark. "Poor, poor, poor boers or whites from cheap suburbs. What do they know better than that!" "Dey wouldn't be queueing up every day like dat if he wasn't doing dem any good." "Nonsense," was all I could say. And the cocks started to crow. Just then he dropped off to sleep. I stood up and took his wife's arm to reassure her that I was going to stay on her side.

Once again, when Karel could stand up, he walked about. He seemed to have recovered his old cheerful mood again, except for thin lines under his eyes to show that pain had kicked him about and marched through him with hobnailed boots on.

"I feel quite right now," he said to me. "Yes, a small slow pain but I t'ink it will go. I must see it goes because I'm sure de boss will not give me more days at de end of de t'irty days. Dey never do dat dese whites. Can't see myself more time in de house if I'm not getting well, and not getting paid neither."

The note of urgency in his voice told me that he must have something on his mind. What, I wondered.

"I'm goin' to watchimball, to Selborne," he said another day.

"I'm takin' a bus."

Two days passed.

"*Hei wena*—You, our friend had a visitor this morning," my wife reported.

'What visitor?"

"A man with a bag in his hand. The sort you see witch doctors carry."

So, just at the time his wife is at work, I thought.

"Are you going to tell his woman?"

I was irritated at her use of "you" as if to disengage herself. No, I'd go and tell him a few hard things and I'd not mince words, I told her.

I did, but he only laughed and said I shouldn't be foolish. The man knew the particular ailment he had described to him. Wasn't fussy either about the fee for opening his bag. Yes man, he had thrown the bones and shells on the floor and spoken to them and they told him how things were. Someone had smeared "some stuff" on his bicycle pedal and it had gone up his leg. Did he say the Jew boss liked him? Yes, very much. Any other black workers at the garage? Two others. Ever had a quarrel with any one of them? Now let's see. No. Was he senior to them? Yes. Some black people have clean hearts, other have black hearts. He could see the way one bone on the fringe was facing. He could hear it talk. He could see one of the garage workers going to an evil doctor to buy black magic.

"It's dere man, T. *die Here weet*—God knows."

"Do you know a saying in my language that it takes a witch to track down another?" I said.

"I don't care if dis one's a witch. It's my leg give me worryness. Man, T, you can see he can't be lying. His face, his eyes are full of wisdom. He took two days to look for de trouble, *two days.* And he talks to me nice, T, takes de trouble, not like dose white watchimballs—bastards at de hospital!"

I left him after his wife had entered.

The next day, instead of taking my sandwiches and tea in the staff room, I cycled home in order to see how Karel was. My mind was full of ugly forebodings...My wife told me that she had taken him lunch as usual but found the "visitor" and so did not stay. Karel did not look worse than the previous day.

When I entered, the "visitor" was not there. But Karel was lying on the bed, his leg stretched out and resting on a tiny bench. Under the bench was a rag, saturated with blood. "What have you done, Karel!" I exclaimed.

"I feel all right, T. De leg will be all right from now. The man dug a hole in the ankle for the poison to come out. Ah!" He released a long heavy sigh. He held his hip with his still-powerful hand, and let it slide down his side, thigh and leg, like one pressing something out of a tube. At the same time he screwed up his face to show how much energy he was putting into the act.

"Ah, T," came the long long sigh again, "I can feel de watchimball—de pain moving out of the hole there. The blood is carrying it out. Oh, shit!" After a pause, he said, "A black man like you, T, can go a long way. A black man has people around him to give him strength. I haven't."

The facial muscles relaxed and his arm hung limp at his side. I looked at the ankle more carefully this time, as much as I dared. The sight of the blood oozing out like that from the inside part of the ankle, and the soaking wet rag on the floor shocked me out of my stupor and confusion. I looked around for a cloth, found one and bandaged the ankle. Without a word, I ran out to my house. I scribbled a note to my headmaster and asked my wife to go and watch over Karel while I went for a doctor a few streets up. He was out making home visits together with his nurse. I was frantic. Move him to hospital twelve miles away? The white hospital four miles away would not touch him. What about transport? Go to the location superintendent to ring the hospital? I gave up. I left a note for the doctor. I went back to wait.

Death came and took him away from us.

While I was helping to clear things up in the house, several days later when Karel's wife was permitted by custom to reorganize their home, she said to me: "I believe Karel once told you about his identity card?" "Yes." She held it in her hand. "I don't know if I should keep it."

My thinking machine seemed to have come to a dead stop and I couldn't utter a word.

"*Ag*, what use is it?" she said.

"Can I *see* it please?"

Below his picture appeared many other bits of information:

NAME: KAREL BENITO ALMEIDA

RACE: COLORED

I gave it back. She tore it to bits.

"Did he tell you about this letter?" She handed it over to me.

It was a letter from the location's white superintendent telling Karel that he would have to leave house No. 35 Mathole Street where he was known to live, and was forbidden from occupying any other house in Corner B as he was registered "colored" and should not be in a "Bantu location."

She took the letter and tore it to bits.

"Soon I know I must leave this house."

"Why? You can tell the superintendent that you are his widow. I know widows are always ejected soon as their men are under the ground. We can help you fight it out." But I knew this was useless heroic talk: the law of the jungle always wins in the end. But that is another story. And in any case, "I was not married to Karel by law," the good woman said.

Born in Pretoria, Es'kia Mphahlele, a remarkable man of letters, attended elementary school locally and high school in Johannesburg. He studied for his Bachelor of Arts degree by correspondence with the University of South Africa and was granted the degree in 1949. In 1956 he was awarded his M.A. degree in English literature and in 1968 was awarded a Ph.D. from the University of Denver, in the USA. He taught in South Africa until 1952 when he was banned from teaching by the Government as a result of campaigning against "Bantu Education" as general secretary of the Teachers Association. During his years of exile he traveled widely in Africa, Europe and the USA, and taught at various universities. He returned to South Africa in 1977 despite being "listed" under the Internal Security Act, which was lifted in 1979. His work includes short stories, plays, novels and essays. In addition to his mother tongue, Es'kiel Mphahlele speaks French, English, Dutch, Spanish and Zulu.

"She wanted to plead to be spared. She could not.
 Fear was choking her."

Accident

BY LINO LEITÃO

I was sitting opposite her in the bus that goes from Dorval to downtown. My head was buried in the *Gazette,* absorbing the editorial   column on Free Trade. I lifted my head to ponder the points the editorial had made. If Free Trade were to become an issue in the coming election, how would I cast my vote? As I was trying to make up my mind, I saw her staring at me. She smiled, as if she had known me before. She was glowing with a smile of recognition. There was no doubt in my mind now that she had known me somewhere. But where? Free Trade was blown away from my mind. I racked my brains. She gently tapped me on my knees and said:

"Don't you know me?"

Her voice did it. It swept the fog away from my mind. I saw her now as vividly as I had known her sixteen years ago in Uganda. How the years have gone by!

"Nancy Price, aren't you?" I bubbled.

Her face was wreathed in smiles. She nodded.

"That's me, all right."

"You've changed."

"Who hasn't? Look at you! You've gone all gray."

"Growing old."

"We all are."

The bus went on stopping at its usual stops. We talked of those good old days. We had a lot to talk about. The bus came to its terminal and we got down. I invited her to McDonald's for coffee and hamburgers.

"Thanks," she said. "I'm in a hurry. I have to be in time for the interview. Looking for a job, you know!"

"I don't have a job, either."

"You too!"

"I'm on my way to see my counselor at the Employment Center."

Nancy Price smiled cynically.

"Here is my number," she said as she was going to catch the other bus. "Let us get together sometime."

I became nostalgic. Nancy Price triggered off memories of Uganda in me. As I watched her disappearing into the crowd, snow started coming down. It's going to be a storm, I thought. I had enough time on me and a few dollars in my pocket, more than enough to buy me a coffee and a hamburger. Coming into McDonald's, I gave my order and sat at the table looking at the brewing snowstorm. My thoughts went to sunny Uganda and Nancy Price.

Nancy Price had come to the Immaculate Conception College of Namirembe when Obote's Government was overthrown in a coup d'etat by Idi Amin. Who doesn't know him? He had become internationally famous as an abhorrent dictator of Uganda. But in the very beginning of his regime the people of Uganda greeted him as their hero. Many Uganda intellectuals praised Amin's regime, never dreaming that he would be a disaster to their country. Nancy Price was also an ardent admirer of Idi Amin then.

Immaculate Conception College was a boarding school. White nuns were in charge of this Catholic institution. It was a girls' college; the daughters of Uganda officials and daughters of other Uganda personages studied here. The teachers were nuns and lay women-teachers brought in from England. John Kiwanuka, a

Muganda and I (I am from India) were the only males who taught in this college. Mother Veronica, the principal of the college, was Irish and had a reputation as an able administrator. At staff meetings, she discussed her administrative strategies and elicited fresh administrative ideas from her staff. Though there was no formal student body in the college at that time, she had Prefects, but nominated through the counsel of her staff. Nancy Price, now a member of the staff of Immaculate Conception College, voiced her opinion at one of the staff meetings. She argued that the nomination of Prefects was yet a democratic process. She was young at that time, she couldn't have been more than twenty-five. Tall, slender, raven black hair, not cut but held in a knot above the nape of her neck, in pony-tail fashion. She was very attractive. She was an American, a white girl, but her skin now had taken a brownish hue, enhancing her sex appeal. Her blue eyes flickered as she talked and she made a kind of impact on the assembly. From John Kiwanuka's looks, I knew he was fascinated by her. Other members of the staff, including myself, didn't say much but observed a kind of respectable silence for Mother Veronica. Mother Veronica considered herself a democrat; with a serene smile and her blue eyes twinkling, she rejected Nancy's arguments. She stated, not to Nancy in particular but to the staff at large, that to serve the people one must know the ins and outs of the people, know the mind and soul of the people. She knew the mind and soul of the Ugandans. She had served in Uganda for many years. She pointed out that she was training the best brains, the future ladies of Uganda, not riff-raff but girls with potential for leadership, chosen of course by her brilliant staff. According to her observation, the nomination of Prefects worked towards the smooth running of the institution. That was what was wanted, not any fanciful ideas, which in the end served only to mess up things. Because she was in a hurry, she said, she had to bring the meeting to a close. Nancy had no chance to refute her. As Mother Veronica was leaving, she gave Nancy a sharp look and then a beatific smile.

Nancy Price wasn't a fool. Through that sharp look and the beatific smile, Nancy claimed that she had a good look at the mental makeup of Mother Veronica, as if they were two wide windows. Mother Veronica was nothing but an outright Colonial, she said, who didn't want to change a thing through education but to subjugate the brain of the collegiate through paternalism, or, in this case, maternalism. She blamed British colonialism in Uganda and elsewhere for creating colonial moral structures like gas chambers and putting the colonized therein to be exterminated. Knowing what Mother Veronica was, she left her alone, but brought the debates at tea-breaks to the staff room. She was a solitary American, the others were from the British Isles, and of course, John Kiwanuka and I were neither American nor British. So we were passive observers. She had a flair for debating and brought in much varied analysis that she had picked up in her readings to show the devastating effects on the colonized. Giving various examples, she demonstrated that the elevated status of the Colonials, in this case the British, was created by exploiting the colonized and thereby bestowing upon them an inferior status. The expatriate British teachers refuted Nancy's hostile attacks on the British Empire. They pointed out that the Britons weren't wholesale exploiters, but human nature being what it is, they weren't perfect. "Who is? No man is perfect. No government is perfect," they said. They accused her of being blind and unable to see the benefits the British Empire had brought, not only to Uganda but to her other colonies too.

"Like what?" Nancy demanded.

"Schools, hospitals, roads, economic development, administrative system, above all law and order and a host of other improvements."

"Hogwash!"

"Of course, you wouldn't understand. They need us, they want our know-how and our technology. And so we are here. Without Western aid these nations have no chance to modernize."

But Nancy, giving statistics, would make her point that the Western aid, the aid of the former Colonial Powers, was not helping Africa a bit. The Western nations developed industrially by exploiting the colonized nations and she argued that they were still perpetuating the same system, except now they had a better grip on them than before, thus making a farce of "independence." She

111

also pointed out that the mechanism of the international economics was still in the hands of the exploiter nations, keeping the former colonies under their thumb. The British teachers weren't dumb, though. Miss Alision Web, with gusto, would argue that the British imperialism was now like a decrepit old man, almost in the grave, and what one should be afraid of now, she would say, was Yankee Imperialism and its economic domination of the world. And she would cite the USA's role in Vietnam and Latin America. Thus, Uncle Sam and John Bull, like two ponderous elephants, tusks locked, wrestled to establish the benevolence of their respective imperialism. Both Miss Alision Web and Nancy Price would cast glances at John Kiwanuka to solicit his support. Neither sought my opinion. I was like a nonentity, a passive listener.

John Kiwanuka hardly said anything. But one day he remarked to the warring debaters, "Exploiters have no moral guilt, no shame. The exploited are uncivilized, brutes and savages to the exploiters. But the exploited isn't an idiot! They know who is the uncivilized and barbarian. Africa is the womb that gave birth to man, and the West is the tomb of man, a destructive force, creator of weapons of doom. It is Africa who knows the pangs of human birth. It is Africa in the end who will restore the moral conscience of man."

They all listened to him, as though his statement was like a revelation that would unfold in the future.

The British teachers set a rumor in motion that Nancy Price was an agent. When asked in whispers whom did she represent, they said she was a CIA agent or she was a double agent spying both for Uncle Sam and Idi Amin. It produced results; Nancy Price was boycotted by the staff and the students. Mother Veronica really believed that Nancy Price was planted by Idi Amin in the institution to keep a watch on the staff and herself.

In the meantime, political conditions worsened. God had appeared to His Excellency Idi Amin in a dream and instructed him to throw the Asians out of Uganda because they were living on the fat of the Africans. The Whites, too, were in trouble. The whole country was in chaos. It was no longer safe both for the Whites and Asians to stay in Uganda (and later on, it wasn't safe for the natives of the country, either). Whites left the country and the Asian

Exodus started from Uganda to the different parts of the world. I landed in Canada. I was in a different world now and Uganda was hardly on my mind, until I happened to meet Nancy Price.

I phoned Nancy Price the following Sunday. She invited me to her apartment that evening. She lived in Lachine, at 32 Ave., not far from Dorval. At about six I arrived at her apartment building. I looked for her name on the Occupants Board but her name wasn't listed. The occupant of her apartment number was "J. Kiwanuka." Did I make a mistake? Hesitantly, I pressed the button. No voice asked me who I was. The main entrance door buzzed, I opened it and went to the elevator. The apartment was 305. The door was ajar. Standing in front of it was a woman dressed in traditional Baganda dress—the Gomisi. She was white.

"I'm sorry," I said rather loudly and apologetically.

"Sorry for what?"

Once again, I recognized Nancy Price through her voice.

"It's you then!"

"Of course, it's me! Who did you expect?"

I looked at her spellbound, surprised at seeing her in that attire. She could have passed for a Muganda woman if she were black and if she had cushioned buttocks.

"Stop admiring me!" she said. "Come in."

I sat on a sofa. As I was looking at a few Baganda crafts displayed on a wall-unit, I heard someone greeting me, a greeting once familiar.

"Sorotiano Sebu."

"Burungi," I said automatically. And before me I saw a black man in a kanzu.

"You?" I exclaimed.

"Yes, me, John Kiwanuka."

He came closer and clasped me in his embrace, as if he had found his long-lost brother. I saw the beaming face of Nancy Price, while I was still held by Kiwanuka. After enough hugging, we all sat. John and Nancy sat on a love seat and exchanged loving glances. I sat on a chair opposite them, dying of curiosity. Nancy's sparkling eyes told me she was eager to tell me their story. I alone, perhaps, would understand and appreciate what they had to tell me. But Nancy excused herself, went into the kitchen and brought in a tray loaded with hot cassava fries. And into my nostrils came the aroma of the steaming matoke. I knew I was in for a treat.

"Well, let us have some beer now," Kiwanuka said and disappeared, coming back with Molsons and mugs.

"John, you forgot the salt and chili-powder shakers," said Nancy.

John brought the salt and chili-powder shakers. He opened the beers and we filled our mugs. There were coffee-colored bark cloth coasters on the table. I took a handful of cassava fries on a paper napkin and sprinkled them with a little salt and splurged the chili-powder on them. I had a sip of beer. All expectant, I looked at Nancy and John. Though Nancy was a good debater, she had no knack at story telling. She rambled a lot and John came to her rescue, as if to put the story on the right track.

"You both married?"

"Of course!" said Nancy.

John Kiwanuka beamed.

"How did all this come about?" I asked.

"I wasn't a coward," said Nancy. "I approved the way His Excellency Idi Amin got rid of the Asians and the White men. They atrophied Uganda morally, intellectually, economically and so on. They were big Bana Kubas who did no physical labor. And the Ugandans who worked for them were looked upon as stupid, lazy, untrustworthy and all that kind of crap. And your race—"

"What about my race?" I asked.

"The kill was made by the Britons and your race was like hyenas gorging on decaying carcasses. That's how your race built their economic securities and empires. What did your race contribute to Uganda? Nothing."

"Hold it a minute there," I said. "You may be right about the Asian presence in Uganda. They might have been parasites as you say. But my race did contribute something."

"And what's that?"

"The national dress that you are wearing," I said. "This dress was introduced by a Goan tailor, called Gomes, hence the name Gomisi. Ask John."

John told her so.

Her mood changed. Both persuaded me to have more cassava fries and more beer. But still her story wasn't coming out. I was really dying to know how Nancy came to get married to John. And in the meantime, the main course was served—matoke with peanut sauce topping it. John excused himself for a while, came in with a bottle and placed it on the table in front of me.

"Waragi!" I exclaimed. "Where on earth did you get it?"

"That's the only thing that I came with from Uganda," he said, "and saved it for many years. But today is a special day and we will have it."

Waragi was on the point of becoming a national drink of Uganda. It was distilled and bottled by the Government. It was a very potent drink, resembling gin. Nancy Price had taken away beer glasses and brought huge goblets for waragi. John poured the waragi into the goblets. I would have preferred mine with a mix, but my host didn't want to dilute the taste of waragi. I sipped mine. My body was on fire. Nancy and John drained theirs in a single gulp and they refilled their goblets. This time, they savored it. We started attacking the matoke. Waragi must have loosened Nancy's soul and tongue. The story poured out.

Uganda cities, like that of Kampala, Jinja and others weren't African as such: they were little Bombays. But now, though they were African, they had become ghost towns, dim and dismal. Nancy Price didn't mind. Asians in Uganda were parasites, they deserved to be thrown out. And those snobbish Britons who lived a leisurely life even after Uganda's independence as though they were still masters and indispensable, deserved to be thrown out as well. Nancy had no sympathy for them. Though the British teachers were given kipandes to stay by His Excellency Idi Amin, they had left. Good riddance! Nancy was the only White who taught at Immaculate Conception College. She was unlike other Whites; she was neither a coward nor an imperialist. She rather enjoyed it when His Excellency Idi Amin made the British residents of Kampala kneel down before him. Didn't the Africans always prostrate before the White Colonials? Tit for tat. And on another occasion, His Excellency Idi Amin sat on a chair and made the

British residents in Uganda carry him to the OAU summit conference at Kampala. Nancy loved the way the Britons were humiliated. Those bastards deserved every bit of it. They were getting it back, what they did to Africans. The common people of Uganda loved it too. He was their hero. Nancy Price admired Idi Amin.

People were murdered in large numbers, thrown in the Nile. Amin was cruel and unpredictable; none knew how his mind worked. Everyone was afraid and frightened but not Nancy Price. She taught at the Immaculate Conception College and on her free time, she traveled in her car to any place in Uganda that she fancied. No Amin soldiers seemed to be bothered with her. She felt no less secure. The bestial behavior of Amin and his regime was just an exaggeration of the Western Press. But one thing she noticed was that the staff and the students at the Immaculate Conception College were frightened of her and that bothered her a lot.

One Sunday morning, she was driving in her car, going to Jinja from Kampala. Near Mabira Forest she was stopped by four army men. They were young, dressed in smart uniforms. They had guns and they were ferocious and arrogant-looking. She didn't panic, she brought the car to a stop by the roadside. They looked into the car, they asked her to open the trunk. They spoke in Swahili. She didn't understand the language. They got angry with her. They asked her again to open the trunk. They were angry, very angry. They were shouting at her, perhaps obscene words in Swahili. But she managed to keep her cool, she wasn't easily frightened. She was not a coward. But when one of the soliders pointed the gun at her, close to her temple, fear grabbed her, shaking her body, and her teeth chattered. These guys mean business—they would shoot her and dump her somewhere in the forest. Nobody would know. The solider stood pointing his gun at her, trigger happy. Anytime now. Her eyes were glazed, begging for mercy. She wanted to plead to be spared. She could not. Fear was choking her. They were gloating over seeing her fear-stricken. They tormented her further. One of the soldiers fired into the air. Poor Nancy thought that she was finished. No more Nancy Price. She slumped on her seat. The intensity of the fear unlocked her bladder. Her urine cascaded, wetting her pantyhose and the driver seat, creating a small puddle under it. The soldiers went hysterical, laughing and thumping on the ground like a bunch of enthusiastic kids, exclaiming loudly in Swahili. A few passersby were courageous enough to see what the fuss was all about. They too laughed loudly. Nancy Price heard them. Never before in her life had she felt so humiliated. These were indeed savages, brutes and barbarians.

In the end, having had their fun, without molesting her they let her go. Nancy drove back to the Immaculate Conception College. She was seething with anger. "Those lousy bastards!" she ranted as she drove. What could she do? Cooling down, she realized how lonely she was. She wasn't safe. Africa was not her home. She wanted to be with people, not any people, white people. But no white people were around. She thought of Mother Veronica and of Alision Web. She needed to talk to someone. Whom? She couldn't talk to the African staff in the College, she had already sensed that they disliked her. If she told them, they would not sympathize with her. They might laugh in her face. She couldn't face another humiliation. She did not know the mental makeup of the Africans, even of the Western-educated ones. She couldn't hold it in any longer. She took a chance, and one day she told it to John Kiwanuka, how the four army men humiliated her. He listened, said not a word and she wasn't sure what was going on in his mind. When she was almost finished telling him, she blurted out with anger, "Those African soldiers are barbarians, brutes, like a troupe of frenzied chimpanzees in the wild. Shouting and calling everyone from the road to see me in that state as if they had discovered something unusual."

"They had," John had said.

She darted a hostile look at him and demanded to know what he meant. He told her very calmly that those African soldiers had discovered that the White could be cowed by the African and that was a discovery for them. Another discovery was seeing her urinating.

"That was a discovery too?" Nancy Price asked.

"Of course."

"Didn't they know that the Whites urinate and do all such biological things like the rest of the animals?"

"In Colonial Africa the Whites weren't animals, they were divinities. Having divine status, they had separate toilets, separate resident areas; they had everything exclusive for themselves, living a leisurely and luxurious life. Nothing has changed much even now. When I was young, I often wondered if the Whites did really urinate and have sex. When the students got pregnant here, Mother Veronica and the White staff looked down upon them as if they were rubbish, as if the Whites did not do such things. And when the nobilities and royalties came from England on official visits to Uganda, they indeed appeared before our eyes like gods and goddesses from heaven. How could such people urinate and have sex? But now, we know better."

Nancy Price was a sensitive woman. For the first time she saw the color of her skin was equated with injustice. Her conscience stirred. She was overcome with emotion. Was it guilt? Was it compassion? Or was it love? She didn't know, but on the spur of the moment, she asked John Kiwanuka to marry her. She almost begged him and, in the end, he consented to take Nancy as his wife.

Our plates were empty; there were no more matoke portions to go around, nor waragi. We had coffee, not from Uganda but from Tanzania. In the end, I took my leave and went home through the snow to put the story on the paper while it was still fresh.

Lino Leitão, born in 1930, was educated in Portuguese and English schools, and attended Karnatak University of India and University of Concordia in Montreal. Trained as a teacher of English and History, he taught for twelve years in Uganda and has taught in other countries. He has published several collections of short stories, many of his stories are about East African Goans. His story "The Marriage" appeared in SSI No. 76.

"Mwansa stood watching them with her hands on her hips and a murmur on her lips as they disappeared into the village."

Fish Soup

BY RICHARD ARMSTRONG

Seven people in a Land Rover pickup seek to buy fresh fish at the mouth of the Kalungwishi River, near Mununga, Zambia.

WE turned off the main road where it crossed the Kalungwishi and followed a dirt track beside the river for about a mile until the solid ground gave way to marsh and the river disappeared into Lake Mweru. The track ended at a beach littered with dugout canoes. A hundred yards ahead five hippos stood in the shade where the river water squeezed past an expanding peninsula of papyrus encroaching its channel; soon the shore would shed this superfluous extension and wind and currents would shift the papyrus island across the lake to another shore or possibly through the outlet and beyond to the Congo mouth, 3000 feet lower and 2900 miles to the west.

We tumbled out of the Land Rover onto scorching earth. The five women, all barefoot, skittered about whimpering until they accepted the searing heat. The river gave no respite; it sucked the baked air from the frizzled shore and kept its own damp coolness to itself.

A knot of silent people sat in the shade of a parked ice truck. From opposite sides of the beach, two languid merchants offered identical selections of soap, soft drinks, bread, and biscuits from crude huts made from grass tied to sticks rammed into the silty-sandy alluvium. In one, an obese woman wearing blouse, skirt, and head covering all made from the same printed cloth with the shades of orange, green, and black used in the national flag, sat on the ground dozing. Her face and neck glistened with sweat and swarmed with flies. The other grocer was a mean looking, hollow-eyed, gray-haired man in cotton shorts and a tattered sleeveless undershirt. He glared at us maliciously as though defying us to come close enough to purchase something. Storks and pelicans were thick at the shoreline scavenging offal where fishermen had cleaned their fish and dried them in the sun.

The beached dugouts were all empty; a powered fiberglass canoe headed up the river toward us. It would bring fish. My girl friend's uncle, her cousin Chibesa, and the three other women walked off toward the furthest point of firm land to intercept the fisherman there, far from the ice truck, so there wouldn't be a conflict with its driver about buying the fish. Mwansa, my girl friend, took off in another direction.

I followed Mwansa toward a flimsy leanto of sticks and grass. An ancient man sat within, smoking a foot-long cigarette rolled in newspaper. He wore a pith helmet, an unbuttoned gray-green military overcoat suitable for a winter campaign in Russia, and brown trousers, much too large for him, cinched around his waist with a thick rope and rolled up at the ankles. When he saw Mwansa headed toward him with me at her tail, his mouth fell open in a grand, one-toothed smile. He clambered to his feet and greeted Mwansa extravagantly in ciBemba then he turned to me with a military salute and said, "Mawnin, suh." With bows and pointing he directed Mwansa to his display of merchandise, a carpet of heavy brown wrapping paper on which he had set out about twenty piles, each containing three flat, brown, resinous, mutilated, smoked fish.

The fish were deep bodied carp, fourteen to sixteen inches long. They had been split down the back, from the upper lip to just before the tail fin, and then laid open for cleaning and smoking. The finished product lay there with its right side occupying the left hand position and its left side occupying the right hand position and the two sides staring .paone another in the face eyeball to eyeball over their common chin.

The flies were oppressive; I wished Mwansa had gone along with the others. She strode up to the old man and asked the price of his smelly fish which she called by name, *mpumbu*.

The man drew his great coat about him and clasped it shut with his left hand; it would be a formal offer; he waved his right hand palm up at his fish. "Madame, these are the last and also the best ones from this year's catch. You know *mpumbu* are only caught for a few days each year. When these are gone there won't be any until next year. The price is only two-and-six for each pile."

Mwansa was only five feet eight but, because of the old man's stoop, she looked down on the top of his tattered pith helmet. She wore an orange, green, and yellow cloth wrapped tightly around her waist and legs and tied stylishly with a bustle in the back. Her hair was braided into a dozen short pigtails which jutted from her scalp at different angles and worked together with the red and yellow headcloth which was elaborately tied to resemble a group of butterflies nestling among the braids. Mwansa lifted one of the fish to her nose and made a bad face: "Hey, old man, you can't charge two-and-six for three of these. Look, they already have maggots. *Soon* there'll be nothing left but bones. I'll give you two-and-six for five."

I had an impulse to jump into the bargaining on the old man's side because I felt sorry for him with his cast-off European clothing and manners and also because I thought Mwansa's remark was harsh and unnecessarily stingy. But I knew that once the old man realized that I spoke ciBemba, he'd make his pitch to me and I'd end up buying all his damned fish out of pity for him even though they looked disgusting and I was sure they were rotten. I remained silent.

The old man was persuasive on his own. "Ayyyeeee, Madame, you'd be stealing my fish. I might as well have not gone fishing. It was terrible work to clean and smoke them. How can I give them away like that? I'll let you have four for three bob."

"Who can pay that much for rotten fish to feed the dogs?" She picked up another one and held it close to the old man's face while she theatrically plucked four wriggling blow fly larvae from the gill cavity and dropped them on his sleeve. "Give us five for three bob and we'll take twenty."

I was astonished that she would consider taking the disgusting things at any price, but the seller held firm. "I can't do that; five are three-and-six."

"OK, old man, you can keep your stinking fish. Let's go, Pollard." She turned away and left me three steps behind as she headed for the river where the others were.

The old man scampered after her. "I'll give you five for three bob and you can pick yourself."

"Forget it, old man, I don't even like *mpumbu*."

The fishing boat was approaching the shore when Mwansa and I reached the others. The lone fisherman began his sales pitch before he beached the boat.

"Look at these! Look at them! Where have you seen such magnificent *mpale*. They're still alive, look!"

For me, the magnificent sight was this short, wiry man's handlebar moustache with the waxed ends jutting four inches to either side. He jumped into the water from the back of his 18-foot fiberglass canoe when it was still thirty feet from shore, oblivious to the soaking this gave his tattered short pants and shirt-tails. He floated the boat closer to shore, then he lifted its bow in both hands and set it on the bank as gently as a mother laying her newborn in a cradle.

Two bench seats divided the canoe into three sections. He had meticulously folded his gillnets into the front section the way he might have seen them on display when he bought them. The large section between the two bench seats contained the *mpale*, a highly regarded fish resembling giant bluegills. These he had artfully arranged in tiers which alternated with layers of fresh lily pads and blossoms. One by one he had positioned the fish with each one pointed in the opposite direction of its two nearest neighbors. The wet lily pads and blossoms separated each layer of fish from the next and blanketed the entire arrangement, protecting it from the sun. Each time live fish at the top of the pile flicked off the garland he would quickly retrieve what had fallen, rinse it in the water, and return it to the top of the pile.

The back section of the boat held everything else, two cans of gasoline for the outboard motor, a tangle of rubber hoses, a tool box, dirty clothes, and a nest of pots encrusted with congealed food. Filling in the voids in this collection of junk were the less marketable fish, walking catfish, spiny squeakers, and enormous, flat-bodied, bottle-nosed suckers.

"How many do you want?" asked the fisherman, drawing back the lily pads to expose a succulent 5-pounder that still quivered. He jabbed his right thumb in its mouth and caught its tail in his left hand and pressed it on Mwansa's uncle: "Ten bob for this one, feel how heavy it is. I can make you a special deal if you buy more than five. You want more than five don't you? Where are you going to find fish as fresh as these? Is this white man going to eat with you? They love this fish; they don't know how to eat most fish that people eat, but this one they do. Just put extra salt on it and fry it; he'll eat it just like people do."

The uncle turned to me and smiled and shrugged his shoulders. He preferred I'd talk a bit in ciBemba before the fisherman embarrassed us all with a cruel remark that he thought I'd not understand. I stepped forward and took the fish and studied it like a French chef. "These fish are beautiful, but your price is too high. That ice truck over there will only give you two-and-six for this fish and he'd give you that even if the fish were half rotten. We'll pay for freshness, but not four times; we'll give you five bob each; what do you say?"

"Five bob, bwana, for fish as fresh as these is unfair unless, of course, you're going to buy ten. If you buy ten, yes, I can make the price be five bob each."

"We'll buy twenty; that's five quid for you, but you have to give us two extra for *imbasela.*"

"Bwana! Even *imbasela!* You know too much. OK. Twenty *mpale* for five quid and I'll give you two for *imbasela.*"

I turned toward Mwansa's uncle for his approval of my bargaining. He beamed like the father of a prodigy and moved next to the fish ready to supervise the selecting. I reached for my wallet.

"No, Pollard. We don't want *mpale.* We want *milobe.*" Mwansa pushed past me out into the water and started tugging on one of the huge, slimy, bottle-nosed suckers buried in the trash at the back of the boat. The fish she was struggling with weighed at least twenty pounds and it was so slimy she couldn't yank it out from underneath the gas can.

"But, Niece, look how beautiful these *mpale* are." Her uncle had that expression of a man watching a herd of hippos destroying his garden. "And I'm sure Mr. Pollard won't like eating *milobe* the same as he would enjoy *mpale.*"

Mwansa let go of the slimy monster and snapped at her uncle: "If you want *mpale,* then buy it with your own money. Pollard and I are going to eat *milobe;* all you have to say is whether or not you're going to take part."

Her uncle certainly didn't have any money. He backed off from the pile of *mpale* and mumbled unconvincingly. "*Milobe* are delicious too." Her Cousin Chibesa's face dropped its smile and turned to stare blankly out across the river; in a whimper so tiny and strained I thought her stomach pain had returned, she echoed her father, "*Milobe* are delicious."

The three other women huddled together in the shallow water where they had been admiring the *mpale.* The youngest and fattest of them stared down at her toes digging in the sand and pebbles and said, speaking quietly to her toes, "It's true; milobe are good fish to eat, too."

The oldest and thinnest of them wrapped her arms tightly around her chest and squeezed out a comment:: "Milobe are not bad if you know how to cook them."

The other one said, "My grandmother knew how to cook *milobe* but she's been dead a long time."

Mwansa ignored them; she was still trying to pull the monster out from under the gas can but it was so slimy and slippery she couldn't hold it. She turned and snapped at me: "Pollard, don't just stand there like a ninny; come here and help me."

I sloshed out to the knee-deep water at the back of the boat where she stood, and stuck my hands into the mess she was pulling at. I jammed my big finger inside the tiny sucker mouth at the end of the snout and hooked my thumb under the operculum. Mwansa had pulled her head cloth off and wrapped it around the fish's tail. Together, we had enough purchase to hoist the gooey thing out of the boat and land it on the sand at the water's edge. Mwansa knelt down next to it and scooped up sand in her hands and smeared it into the slime to make it easier to handle. She looked up at me, "If you don't mind, I think we should buy another one. These people are acting silly now, but when it's time to eat they'll be hungry."

We left there with two twenty-pound *milobe*.

Nobody talked on the drive back to the village. The four women in the back couldn't huddle together to talk as before since the two huge fish occupied the entire center portion of the rear section and they had to separate from one another and hang over the edges to protect their clothing from the slime. Mwansa's uncle wrapped his arms around his chest and planted his forehead on the window to his side. Mwansa sat next to me with her hands folded in her lap and her lip poked out. Neither would talk to me.

When we reached the cassava field below the village, the others jumped out of the Land Rover and skooted off up the hill like they were in a race. Mwansa stood watching them with her hands on her hips and a murmur on her lips as they disappeared into the village. When they were finally gone, she shouted, "Go ahead and run, you dogs."

I shouldered one fish, no longer slimy because of the sand, and she balanced the other one on top of her head. When we entered the village at the top of the hill, the others were out of sight. Mwansa halted between the houses and turned all the way around slowly in tiny steps so she could look everywhere without twisting her neck and possibly losing the fish from on top of it.

"Stupid cows, no one is going to help cook these fish. Well, I don't need them; they'd spoil the food, anyway. Let's put the fish in the shade in the *nsaka*. I'll go for water and a knife."

She dropped her fish on the dirt floor of the *nsaka,* a round gazebo with half-walls of poles and mud and a thatched roof, and stormed off haranguing any audience only she could see with a tirade of anatomy and bodily functions for which I didn't even know English equivalents. She charged back with a basin of water, a knife and a five-gallon cooking pot, then tore off again with a basket, and twisted and yanked, from trees within the village, five green mangoes, a large unripe papaya, two lemons, and a handful of fiery chiles. She set the basket of fruit down next to me in the *nsaka* and went off again to a clump of bamboo to gather branches. She selected pencil thick shoots and cocked her ear to catch the snap as she broke each one off the trunk. She returned to the *nsaka* with a dozen branches wedged in her armpit. She withdrew them one by one to strip the leaves and give them a final snap to make them fit her cooking pot. Snapping and stripping the sticks tranquilized her. When she finished, she showed a faint smile. She built up a net of bamboo branches in the bottom of the pot and set it aside.

She squatted beside one of the huge fish and started scraping. "I don't need them to help me; the fish will be better because I did it by myself. See how it is living in a village? They don't want you to choose what to do by yourself even if you know what you want. What you want by yourself doesn't count; what you think by yourself doesn't mean anything; what you think by yourself is like the noise a river makes spilling over the rocks; it doesn't do anything. You're only supposed to want what the big mouths want. Well, I've got a big mouth too and they can go to hell."

She gutted, gilled, and definned the fish and cut off their ridiculous heads and packed them into the bottom of the pot with chunks of fruit and a handful of rock salt. The rest of the fish she chopped into three-inch sections which she stacked neatly on top of the heads, together with fruit and chiles and an occasional handful of salt, until the five-gallon cooking pot was brimful. She covered it and weighted the cover down with an old tire rim and set it on a bed of hot coals and heaped dirt and ashes around it to seal the heat in.

In the dusking hour, two hours later, I watched Mwansa slip over to one of the other houses and tap tentatively on the door: "Hello in there, the fish are done and now I'm going to prepare *ubwali*. Please let me use the big pot so I can cook enough for everyone."

After knocking and calling she knelt before the door, folded her hands in her lap, and stared down at them. The door jerked open and a hand thrust a huge, black pot at her and snapped back inside; the door slammed shut.

I watched from the curious handmade chair in the *nsaka* where I had been dozing since she finished preparing the fish. Four gnarled tree branches were lashed together at about their midpoints. Two of the poles curved up above the binding like a pair of horns, and the other two projected out like tusks. Below the binding, all four poles splayed out giving the thing a base. A hammock, made of animal skins stitched together with leather thongs, hung between the horns and the tusks. I reclined in it with my legs straddling the tusks, my head lolling on the hammock, and a clay jar full of banana wine cradled in my lap.

I perked up at the aroma from the fish pot when Mwansa plucked it from the hearth and set it in the *nsaka* next to me. Knowing what had gone into the pot couldn't help me identify some of the subtler scents. I drained my jar of wine and she took it away and refilled it. Now I was impatient to eat.

Mwansa built up the cooking fire with a bundle of twigs and a few stout branches and put the big black pot half full of water on to heat. She sat next to the fire singing softly and probing in the ashes with a stick. Someone cursed fiercely in one of the houses. A dog squealed in pain. A door flew open. The dog tumbled out yelping and hobbling on two legs. More curses and a thrown shoe thudded against its side. The door slammed shut. Mwansa looked up and whistled. The whimpering dog limped nearby than crawled up to her on its belly and put its head on her lap.

When the water steamed and rumbled, she stirred two pounds of corn meal into half a gallon of cold water in a sauce pan, then mixed it into the hot water in the larger pot and covered it. Twenty minutes later she snatched the cover off four gallons of boiling porridge. She took a *munko,* a large hand-carved wooden spoon, and stirred down the boil, then smothered it with another pound of corn meal. The mass congealed and she strained to hold the pot down with her left hand while she beat furiously with the *munko* in her right. When the mass in the pot was about to solidify, she snatched it off the fire and scooped the stiff porridge into three enameled basins.

Mwansa finished cooking, exhausted and soaked with sweat. She stood for a moment at the entrance of the *nsaka* leaning against a post and staring dejectedly at the closed doors of the two nearest houses. Without facing me she said, "I need to go behind the house to wash and change out of these sweaty clothes. Can I give you some more wine before I go?"

She came back with a basin of water for hand washing, then she served me from a tray with the smallest dish of *ubwali* and a plate of fish and soup. She sat on the ground next to me sadly considering the two large basins of *ubwali* remaining and the huge pot of fish. "I cooked all this food but I don't think the others will come to eat it."

I thought that was preposterous. "They must be hungry and don't you think they can smell it? If they can smell it, they'll have to come eat it because it smells so good."

"That's what you think, but one of them would probably say it smells like urine. People see or smell according to what they know ought to be true and right now they think that whatever I do ought to be disgusting because they're mad at me."

I scooped up a lump of the steamy *ubwali* with my fingers. I kneaded it with my finger tips for a moment until it cooled. I never could eat my *ubwali* the way most people did, from plate to soup to mouth, still scalding hot. I had to cool it down and roll it into a ball in my palm and then flatten it into a disk that could scoop up an extra measure of soup. At last, I plopped it into the soup on my plate, then sucked it into my mouth. "Mwansa, this soup is delicious." I plucked a piece of fish off the pile on my plate; the bones fell out cleanly as I picked it up. At first I nibbled, biting off a small chunk and pressing it with my tongue for a moment against the roof of my mouth. Light, flaky, sensuous; I wolfed down the rest. "This is even better than the aroma; you have to call the others."

She walked over to the house where she had borrowed the pot earlier, knelt in front of the door, and called out, "Hello, in there. I finished cooking *ubwali*. Please come to eat." She ran back to where I sat in the furthest part of the *nsaka* and kneeled on the ground next to me and began to nibble unenthusiastically at the food on my tray.

Twenty minutes passed. I continued to eat and to rave to her about her cooking, but I was nearly full and she had barely eaten anything. Maybe the best fish dish I had ever eaten would spoil because of sour attitudes. Then the old, thin woman left her house scowling and scuffed her way over to the *nsaka*. She never acknowledged us; she washed her hands, filled a small plate with the fish, and sat down next to one of the large basins full of *ubwali*.

The old woman ate a few morsels, then stood and returned to her house without any comment and still scowling. She returned, followed by the three other women and the uncle. Chibesa fixed a plate of fish for her father and he took one of the bowls of *ubwali* for himself and came to the back of the *nsaka* where Mwansa and I sat. The women huddled around the biggest basin of *ubwali* and the kettle of fish. The uncle spoke first, "I didn't know you could cook *milobe* like this. It's good."

"Cousin, I hope you will show me how to cook fish like this." That was Chibesa.

The young, fat woman said, "*Milobe* is really the best kind of fish there is."

The old, thin woman said, "Of course, everyone knows that.

129

 *Born in 1936, in Massachusetts, Richard Armstrong earned his Ph.D. in Zoology in 1969, in California. He is a consulting scientist and an author. In 1988 he and his wife completed building a home in her native village in rural Zambia, where they plan to return soon. He is scheduled to edit his work about African spiritual beliefs and to finish a historical novel set in Zambia.*

"Trofimov had mustered all his determination,
as though for a parachute jump, and
invited Sivana for a dance."

Thou Shalt Not Make...

BY VICTORIA TOKAREVA

HIS wife was constantly slimming and so there was never any bread in the house. In the morning Trofimov would open the wooden breadbin, see stale, moldy hunks covered with tiny ants and it would seem to him that these hunks were like his whole life: cheerless and, in a sense, offensive.

His wife would come into the kitchen with a guilty expression and say: "Couldn't you buy some yourself? You know that I don't eat carbohydrates."

"But you don't live here alone," Trofimov would remind her.

"I do," she would object gently. "You don't notice me even when I'm right in front of you."

It was true. Trofimov was in love with another woman. Her name was Silvana and she lived in Rome. There was no future or almost no future for them. There was only the past and, speaking frankly, even that past concerned Trofimov alone.

Trofimov had seen Silvana in the Italian film *All About Her*. She played the principal part and no other films with her had been shown in Moscow. Perhaps Silvana had left the cinema altogether, or perhaps she did appear in films, but these films were never imported. Trofimov saw her only once. He was fifteen at that time—an eighth-form pupil. Silvana appeared on the screen, large, splendid and blue-blooded like a thoroughbred horse. She had enormous, unnaturally beautiful eyes and teeth—such white and even teeth do not exist in nature because nature is not a jeweler and allows flaws and defects. Silvana was perfection itself, a triumph of nature. She was embracing an ordinary, absolutely unremarkable bloke, pressing him against her with her large white arms. Then she wept, fell into despair, and tears—also large and sparkling like diamonds—welled in her beautiful eyes and rolled down her cheeks.

Fifteen is an impressionable age. Silvana had given Trofimov a shock, literally and figuratively speaking. He felt shivery and was unable to get up.

"Are you ill, or something?" his friend and classmate, Kirka Dodolev asked him.

Trofimov did not reply. He could not speak. For some reason his throat had become sore. Silvana had invaded him like an infection, like the *staphilococcus aureus,* which, according to doctors, is extremely difficult, almost impossible to drive out of the organism. It settles there for good. Sometimes it lies low in the man, and then it may seem that it is not there at all. But it *is* there. And it makes itself felt at the most inappropriate moments.

On finishing school Trofimov entered the Department of Journalism at the university, secretly hoping that he would be sent to Italy, where he would interview Silvana. Everything would begin with that interview. Trofimov studied foreign languages—Italian, English and Japanese. Perhaps, Silvana would want to speak to him in Japanese?

Every language is like its native speakers: when immersing himself in the sound of foreign words, Trofimov sensed foreigners by ear, becoming now a little British, now a little Japanese.

To be sent to Italy, one had to be a good journalist, not just a journalist. Trofimov studiously learned many diverse subjects, turning from a layabout into a hard-working fellow right before his parents' eyes. Later, the need to work hard turned into a habit and he never became a layabout again.

At the end of the third year at the university, the twenty-year-old Trofimov won the first prize from the *Smena* magazine for the best essay and his photograph was printed on the last page. The photograph was dark and not a good likeness but still, it was his face which had appeared in several thousands of copies. Trofimov's face seemed to have separated from him and it now belonged to all humanity. This brought him nearer to Silvana. They were almost on a par with each other now. He gathered together all the third-year students and they went to a restaurant to celebrate the event. They enjoyed themselves thoroughly and noisily. Life held out to each a firm promise of fame, love and immortality. But suddenly at the height of the celebration Trofimov felt a complete emptiness. Evidently the *staphilococcus aureus* had got out of the dark corners of his organism and set off a journey along the main thoroughfares. Trofimov suddenly realized how trifling the prize from the *Smena* magazine and the royalties of forty old roubles were for Silvana. Everything lost its meaning for him. He went out of his way to hide his mood from his friends in order not to spoil the party. But if he had tried to explain to them what was happening to him, they would not have understood him and might even have given him a good beating.

After the first prize Trofimov received a second one—the Gold Bull Prize—in Bulgaria. Then a U.N. prize. And then he stopped counting the prizes. He had simply become a good journalist, a "gold pen," as he was called jokingly. But it was such a trifle for Silvana...

Trofimov did not fall in love and marry for a long time because all the candidates were like small puddles or streams or at best rivers in comparison with an ocean. His love for Silvana made Trofimov unapproachable by other women. And unapproachableness embellishes not only women but men as well. Trofimov was handsome and looked enigmatic and disappointed, like Lermontov. Women fell at his feet in the literal and figurative senses of the word. One of them fell at his feet right on a skating rink, risking injury because Trofimov was running on the ice at a speed of 40 miles an hour, like a Pobeda car. Pobeda cars are no longer made, but at that time they were very popular. Trofimov stumbled against the girl and fell. In the end he had to see her home. The girl's name was Galya. All the girls were Galyas then, just as all are Natashas now. In her flat Galya offered Trofimov a cup of tea. At tea she confessed that she had fallen intentionally and not accidentally. She simply could no longer bear unrequited love and was prepared to die by the hand, or rather by the foot, of the man she loved. It turned out that Galya had been in love with him since the eighth form at school and all the way through university. They had studied at the same school, but in different forms; then at the same university, but in different departments. So Trofimov did not remember, or practically did not remember her. For him entire womankind was divided into two halves: Silvana and Not-Silvana. The first half consisted of a single woman, whereas the second comprised all the others. Since he was not destined to be married to Silvana, any other woman from the second half could be his wife. So why not Galya if she wanted it so much?

The wedding was celebrated in Galya's flat. There were so many people that there was hardly any room to swing a cat. There were not enough places at the table for everybody, so they ate in two shifts like in an overcrowded Young Pioneer camp. But all the same the party was noisy and extremely jolly.

Galya was mad with happiness and because of her tight shoes. She had large feet—size thirty-nine—and was ashamed of it, so she had put on shoes two sizes too small for her feet to look more elegant. At that time it was considered chic to have small feet. Many years later Galya bought shoes a size too large, so that walking should be more comfortable, and wore size forty and not thirty-nine. And she was indifferent to the opinion of the people around. Although neither then nor now did the people around pay attention to what size shoes she was wearing. Everything lay in herself. Young Age differs from Not-Young Age in its dependence on the opinions of others.

No one noticed Galya's sacrifice at the wedding either: they all were enjoying themselves for all they were worth, and Galya felt like the stepmother's daughter who had thrust her foot into the crystal shoe. In the end she simply took off the shoes and walked in her stockings. Somebody had broken a glass. Galya stepped on a splinter and cut her foot. Trofimov rushed for a towel, knelt in front of her, and at that moment he felt the familiar emptiness. He was kneeling not in front of Silvana...She remained in Rome with her husband—not Trofimov, but some millionaire, the owner of factories which manufactured ball-point pens and digital watches and clocks, travel agencies, hotels and many other establishments—whereas he, Trofimov, was celebrating his wedding in a shared flat, with cod in tomato sauce, beetroot and potato salad, jellied minced meat, Galya in shoes that were too small for her, and blood on his hands, as though he had himself murdered his dream.

The guests joined their hands, forming a ring. And Trofimov stood on his knees in the center of the dancing ring, falling into the abyss of loneliness.

Then he got himself drunk and went to sleep in the lavatory. No one could get in, so they had to break down the door.

Then everything went in a whirl. The fifties were followed by the sixties and then by the seventies. In the sixties there was a campaign for the reclamation of virgin and fallow lands. Composers wrote songs, poets composed verse, and journalists wrote articles. "The road goes on without end; greetings to you, fallow land!" In the seventies the building of the Baikal-Amur Railway began. On television screens a middle-aged double-chinned singer chanted: "Baik-kall-Am-mur is the song of mill-lions."

Trofimov marched in step with his country; he visited the virgin land reclamation areas and the Baikal-Amur Railway construction sites. And when oil had been discovered in Tyumen, he flew to Lake Samotlor, in which there was no fish. No fish lived there. Did not want to. Trofimov flew in a helicopter and from above he saw yellow bubbling swamps, which looked like boils on the earth's body. However, scientists maintained that swamps were necessary for nature, even indispensible, and the draining of them would mean forceful interference with nature, for which it might take revenge later. Nature knows best what it needs and what it does not need. And man was not God, but part of nature, the same as, say, a swamp.

Trofimov marched in step with his time, sometimes arguing with his time, and occasionally overtaking his time, which is a sign of genius. A man of genius differs from an ordinary man in that he is one hundred—and sometimes two hundred—years ahead of his time.

He had not managed to go to Italy. And Silvana did not come to Moscow. Trofimov spoke English and Japanese with other people. However, Silvana, or rather his love for her, had left him a few habits: to work hard, not to pay attention to women, that is, not to be a womanizer, and not to hide from life behind women's backs.

Galya had every reason to consider herself a happy woman. Reasons there were, happiness there was not. She had captured Trofimov's body, but had failed to capture his heart, and did not know how to do that. She possessed Trofimov and at the same time did not possess him. Contradictions clashed within Galya's heart. It made her grow fat, and she was permanently on a diet. She tortured herself with hunger, always going hungry and cheerless. How could this be called happiness?

In addition to Trofimov's capacity for work and his integrity, Silvana had left in him a feeling of a purposeless life. The *staphilococcus aureus* had grown older together with him and now traveled through the thoroughfares of his organism more rarely and not so brazenly. Still, it was there. Trofimov knew it and felt it to be a flaw. Today the term "complex" is in fashion. Trofimov had a Silvana complex. He feared that it might be noticed and so hid his complex behind conceitedness. Many people believed Trofimov to be haughty.

The seventies were followed by the eighties. Italian neo-realism was a thing of the past. The founder of neo-realism, Cesare Zavattini, had died. Gina Lollobrigida had taken up photography. New stars—Stefania Sandrelli and then Ornella Muti—had replaced the old ones. But none of them could impress Trofimov as forcefully as Silvana had. Perhaps it was because fifteen is an impressionable age, while forty-five is not. The only thing that can shock you at forty-five is a direct, imminent threat to your life. For example, you open your door and see a pistol aimed at you, as in Italian political thrillers of recent years. With age man works out an adaptability to all the other impressions and emotions. But another reason for loyalty is also possible. Trofimov was a stable man. Stability is a feature of a person's nature, a variety of decency. Trofimov did not like moving the furniture in their flat, wore the same overcoat for many years, and did not change his employment. He had married Galya once and for all, and he loved only one woman—Silvana. He had gone on his holiday in the same month—July—and had had one and the same friend—Kirka Dodolev—with whom he had been friends since their sixth year at school and with whom years ago he saw the film *All about Her*. And it was the same Kirka Dodolev and no one else who announced that his holiday would have to be put off from July to August because in July there would be an international film festival in Moscow and among others the Italian actress, Silvana, would be coming to Moscow.

Silvana was coming to Moscow...Trofimov's dream was to come true. The dream had aged a little, but it was still alive.

Kirka Dodolev told him the news over the telephone. He expected a reaction, but Trofimov was silent. His throat immediately became very sore. He could not speak. He replaced the receiver and went home at once. It so happened that in his flat the water tap in the kitchen started leaking and water kept on dripping, making a maddening sound. The sound echoed in his head like the tapping of a woodpecker. He wrapped his throat and called a plumber. It seemed to him that there was some mysterious connection between water, Silvana and his health. But the plumber, Vitali, whom he had called, gave everything quite a materialistic explanation: the washer in the tap had worn out. It had to be replaced.

"Have you got a washer?" Trofimov asked.

"Of course I have."

Vitali opened his tool box and took a rubber washer from it.

"Here it is." He showed the washer to Trofimov and began to take the tap apart.

Trofimov was astonished. He was used to a different system of relations between a plumber and a tenant. In this old system the plumber would say that washers had not been available in shops for over a year and that there was no way of getting them, but he would be able to buy one from a plumber he knew. He himself did not want any cash, but the efforts of others had to be remunerated. The tenant would beg like a dog wagging its tail and pay five roubles for what cost eleven copecks.

Vitali was different. Either a new generation of plumbers had grown or Vitali simply was an honest fellow and it had nothing to do with any generation.

"How old are you?" Trofimov asked.

"Forty-five," said Vitali. "Why?"

Trofimov was surprised. Vitali looked like a bedraggled vocational training school student doing practical work. General Gremin, whom Tatiana Larina had married, was forty-five and Pushkin regarded him as an old man "with gray hair." Either the conditions of life in the twentieth century had changed owing to the technological progress and people did not wear themselves out by the time they reached fifty, or the generation born before the war or at the very beginning of the war bore the stamp of infantilism, or youthful looks were Vitali's personal quality rooted in his genetic code. Honesty and youthful looks.

If Vitali were washed clean and dressed in better clothes, his appearance would not be different from that of a corresponding member of the Academy of Sciences, or a traveler, or a highway robber.

One day Trofimov watched a television program in which a large photo portrait was displayed before a number of participants who were told that it was a portrait of a scientist of international renown and were asked to characterize him on the basis of his outward appearance. The participants noted his intellect, modesty, concentration, and high intelligence. Then the chairman confessed that the man was not a scientist, but a habitual criminal, and asked the participants to take a closer look. They looked and they all found in the same face signs of mental deficiency, dullness and cruelty. Then the chairman apologized and said that it was really a scientist, a theoretical physicist, and asked the participants to look again. And again the face revealed intellect, strength and intelligence. The most interesting thing was that Trofimov also perceived the portrait in accordance with what eyes he looked at it with. So everything depended on the suggestion.

Trofimov looked at Vitali favorably. He even wanted to tell him about the festival and Silvana. Trofimov was overflowing with this important event and he felt an urge to unburden himself. It was impossible to unburden himself to his wife: one was not supposed to talk with one's wife about other women. It was likewise impossible to talk with his son, who was at an age when all relations between people had no nuances: they were specific and were called by specific words. And what words could be found for the relations between Trofimov and Silvana...His son would simply be unable to understand him. So he had to trust an absolute stranger.

"There'll be a festival in July," Trofimov said as though he attached no importance to it.

Vitali stopped working and looked out of the window. It was snowing outside. July was far off. He turned to the sink again and resumed his work without saying anything.

"The press bar will be open all night." Trofimov thought he and Silvana might sit at the same table.

"Where?" Vitali asked unexpectedly.

"What 'where?'" Trofimov did not understand.

"That press bar. Where will it be?"

"At the Moskva Hotel. Why?"

"No reason," said Vitali.

"Have you seen the film *All about Her?* It was on in the fifties. You must remember."

"Mmmm," said Vitali.

"Have you seen it?" Trofimov insisted. It was an important point.

"Don't remember."

"Then you haven't seen it. Or else you'd have remembered it. There was an actress there...She will be coming to the festival."

"She must be an old woman by now," Vitali said.

"Why?" Trofimov was taken aback.

"The film was on in the fifties and now it's the eighties. So work it out yourself. She must be fifty or even over sixty."

For the first time in all these years Trofimov realized that time was an objective factor: it slipped by him and it slipped by Silvana as well. Only two categories of people never got older: dead people and people of one's dreams. And yet Trofimov stared at Vitali with an expressionless face. Meanwhile Vitali calmly finished his work and checked the result. The tap was tight and turned easily, and the washer stopped the flow reliably.

"It's O.K.," said Vitali and began to put his tools into the box.

Trofimov came to and took out his wallet. Previously such work was remunerated by one rouble, but now one rouble was not worth much. You couldn't buy anything with one rouble. Trofimov thought: How much should he give Vitali? Three roubles or five? Five was too much. It could corrupt the workman: he would not want to do anything without a tip and lose his human dignity. The concept "working man's pride" had become purely speculative. And much of the blame for it lay at the door of the intelligentsia. A social stratum must be in the vanguard of society and not flirt with a class and offer it three-rouble notes.

Thinking thus, Trofimov took out a three-rouble note and offered it to Vitali.

"No," the plumber refused.

"Why?" Trofimov was genuinely surprised.

"What for? I get my wages."

"Is your house maintenance service office competing for an honorary title?" Trofimov tried to guess.

"What honorary title?" Vitali did not understand.

"A Communist Labor Brigade."

"Personally I don't compete for any title. I work and that's all."

"Are there many people like you in your organization?" Trofimov asked.

"I'm the only one like me. Each person is unique. Why do people like to generalize?"

Trofimov felt ashamed of the three roubles and said:

"Well, thanks a lot...If I can do something for you, I'll be glad to oblige."

"I'd like to visit the press bar, even just once," Vitali confessed.

It was snowing outside. July was far off and at that moment Trofimov was eager to please Vitali.

"Of course!" he said enthusiastically. "With pleasure..."

Vitali left and Trofimov fell to thinking. The borderline between the classes was disappearing. Today it was already impossible to tell a peasant from a worker, and a worker from an intellectual. Every one read books, watched television and wore jeans, which were available in the shops. Was that good or bad? He had no straightforward answer to this question and decided to think it out. It could provide an interesting topic for a special investigation.

In the press bar one was allowed to smoke. The room was not large and smoke was hanging there in layers, like fleecy clouds. In that smoke floated women in low-necked dresses and jewelry. It was impossible to tell a Soviet woman from her foreign counterpart. They all seemed to be foreigners. True, the trained eyes of the waiters could tell the difference at a glance.

Through the smoke screen Trofimov saw himself in a mirror. Not only was he indistinguishable from the foreigners, but he also looked even more *foreign*; slim and elegant, in his white hopsack suit with a crimson handkerchief showing from his breast pocket and a matching crimson tie, exuding the scent of expensive tobacco and perfume.

He saw Silvana at once. She was sitting at a table by the wall and was a head taller than the people round her. She was as large, splendid and brilliant as she had been thirty years before. Beside her—Trofimov noticed it also at once—sat a ubiquitous fellow nicknamed Bow. His nickname came from his trade: a ladies' tailor. Bow, who was a handsome swindler, was always in the thick of events. Trofimov could dream of sitting near Silvana all his life, but Bow was actually sitting beside her, pouring out champagne for her into a sturdy wine glass. On the other side of her sat a foreigner, a representative of some commercial firm, who worked in Moscow. Perhaps he was acting as an interpreter. This businessman spent nine months a year in Moscow, and the rest of the time in airplanes, flying from one country to another. He was short, with a handsome face and, by Soviet standards, was fabulously rich. By Western standards he was simply rich. He was a great success with women. This might be the reason that had kept him in Moscow for so long. Russian women enjoy a high reputation in the West. They are sincere, romantic, and it is easier to make them happy.

Bow saw Trofimov and beckoned to him. So far things were working out well.

On approaching the table, Trofimov saw a famous Soviet film director sitting there. He was obviously bored. His face wore the expression of a man suffering from forced inaction. Such faces are often seen at railway stations.

Trofimov avoided looking at Silvana. He kept putting off that moment. He was afraid of it. However, now it had become impossible to put it off any longer.

"Let me introduce you," Bow began cheerfully. "This is the Italian actress...."

"I know," Trofimov interrupted him and looked straight at Silvana. He felt as though he had been scalded.

"And this is a Soviet journalist. A wolf. A superwolf," Bow introduced Trofimov.

The businessman translated. Silvana asked something: probably she did not understand the meaning of *superwolf.*

"A fine journalist," Bow explained. "A *grande professore.*"

Silvana nodded slightly and extended her large white hand to Trofimov. He looked at that extended hand and did not dare to touch it.

"Do sit down. Why are you standing?" said Bow in surprise.

The table was for six and only four seats had been taken. Two seats were vacant. Bow was selecting his *milieu.* To have Trofimov at his table was prestigious enough. Not Fellini, of course, but still...Bow took scrupulous care of his *milieu,* as all upstarts do.

The film director put the glass of champagne into Silvana's outstretched hand. She did not understand why the *grand professore* did not shake hands with her, but perhaps it was a custom with Russians...She brought the glass to her divine lips and regarded Trofimov for some time with her horsy eyes. He felt as though he were standing in flames.

"Do take a seat!" Bow demanded.

Trofimov pulled out a chair in order to sit down, but at that moment a man wearing a band round his sleeve approached him.

"Someone is asking for you."

"Me?" Trofimov was surprised.

"Yes, you," said the man on duty and pointed to the door.

Trofimov looked in the direction indicated, but could see nothing through the smoke screen.

"Just a moment," Trofimov looked at Silvana and added, "*Uno moment,*"

Silvana nodded almost imperceptibly. She behaved like a professional beauty. That *was* her profession: a beauty. A woman of that profession will not entertain people at a table with conversation and will not put her hand on the arm of the person she is talking to to show her trust and liking. She does not need that. To talk and to put her hand on somebody's arm is a means of rousing his interest, which is a kind of offensive. But a beauty is always in the state of active defense and, as a means of defense, she builds a wall between herself and the surrounding world. This wall is transparent, but it is there. And Trofimov was up against it although he had not exchanged even a couple of words with Silvana. This filled his heart with coldness and anxiety.

"Just a moment," he said a third time and followed the man on duty.

Near the door the smoke was not so dense and he saw the plumber, Vitali, being prevented from entering by two hefty fellows. Vitali was wearing a gray work jacket and a flat imitation suede reddish cap. Apparently he had been on night shift, nobody had needed him, he had become tired of sitting in an empty house maintenance service office and so he went to the press bar, as he and Trofimov had agreed last February.

"There he is!" Vitali shouted, recognizing Trofimov, who was approaching the door. "I told you and you didn't believe me," he reproached the men on duty. "Tell them!" he said to Trofimov.

Trofimov was taken aback. Vitali had come at a very inappropriate moment. In the words of the saying, Trofimov needed him as badly as a fish needs an umbrella. But Vitali did not know it. He did not suspect he was the umbrella of the saying. He had been invited and he came, as agreed.

"Well, I'm off," he said to the men on duty and squeezed himself into the bar. "Thanks for inviting me."

He came up to Trofimov, looked round and said: "Some smoke! Well, where shall we sit?"

From behind the smoke screen Bow appeared and said: "Are you making yourself scarce?"

"No, I'm not," Trofimov replied.

"Have you any money on you?"

"Yes."

"Then let's go. It's not very polite."

Trofimov followed Bow, and Vitali followed Trofimov.

Everybody sat down at the table. Vitali sat between Trofimov and the film director. Silvana looked at Vitali inquiringly since he was new and rather incongruous with the prevailing style.

"I'm his friend," Vitali introduced himself and patted Trofimov on the shoulder.

"Yes," Trofimov confirmed and said unexpectedly even to himself. "He is a Russian Alain Bombard."

"Oh!" Silvana was astonished, forgetting for a moment that she was a professional beauty. "*C'è impossibile!*"

"Yes, it is," Trofimov insisted. "He's our Alain Bombard."

"And who's that?" Vitali whispered to him.

"She's an Italian," Trofimov replied softly.

"Not her, that bloke you've compared me with."

"Later," Trofimov said.

"Has the same experiment been made in the Soviet Union?" The businessman was surprised.

"Of course. We don't lag behind in anything," Trofimov said proudly.

"I never said you did," the businessman said defensively.

"Were you afraid?" asked Bow. He was probably trying to apply that variant to himself.

"Say that you were," Trofimov advised in a whisper.

"And what do you think? I was terribly afraid." Vitali played up convincingly.

"And it's precisely that which is important," the film director said. "If one is not afraid, there's no heroism."

Suddenly the businessman invited Silvana to dance. She got up. She was wearing a silk tea-rose pink dress. A bitterish jasmine scent wafted past Trofimov.

Silvana followed the businessman into the midst of the dancers. He barely reached her elbow. But perhaps this was considered unimportant in the West. If one was rich, one could be even knee high.

"Some mare!" said Vitali, meaning Silvana.

Bow invited a blonde as small and frail as Thumbelina.

"Oh," Vitali approved. "You could put 'er in your pocket."

Trofimov took no offense at Vitali's remark about Silvana. On the contrary, by disparagingly calling Silvana a "mare" he had humanized her. He shortened the distance separating the inaccessible Silvana from the ordinary Trofimov, as it were. In the final analysis all people were people, and every person a person. And not more than that.

"You could've changed at least," Trofimov remarked good-naturedly.

"What for?" Vitali was surprised. "I'm quite comfortable as I am."

"You may be comfortable. You don't see yourself. But others aren't comfortable. They see you."

"Conventions," Vitali said carelessly. "Who's that bloke?"

"Which one?" Trofimov did not understand.

"Who you compared me with."

"Alain Bombard," Trofimov pronounced clearly.

"Is he a Tartar?"

"A Frenchman. He crossed an ocean in an inflatable boat."

"What for?"

"To test human possibilities."

"What's that?"

"To understand what a man can do if he's left alone on an ocean."

"And what can he do?"

"He may die. And he may survive. It depends on himself."

"And what if that French fellow had been gobbled up by sharks?"

"He might've been. It was a risk."

"But what for? For the sake of what?"

"You've already asked that," Trofimov reminded. "He wanted to prove that people who are shipwrecked die of fear and of nothing but fear. He's proved that if one doesn't get scared, one may survive, eating raw fish and drinking sea water."

"Was he shipwrecked?"

"No. He wasn't."

"Then why did he do all that?"

"He didn't do it for himself. For others. He wanted to prove that there's a way out of any situation."

"I see..." Vitali became thoughtful. "Was he paid for that?"

"I don't know. Perhaps he was, perhaps he wasn't. That's not the point."

"What is the point?"

"The idea."

"And what is an idea?"

"Don't you know?"

"I do. But I want to know the opinion of a cultured man."

"Idea is an abstract category, like dream or hope."

"And love?"

"If it is unrequited," Trofimov answered and became thoughtful himself.

Requited love turns into children, which means that it is already matter and not an abstraction. Whereas unrequited love shines high above life like a dream. Like everything and nothing.

"I'm bored," the film director said suddenly. "I can only work. I don't know how to live. And that is also a talent—knowing how to live."

Vitali did not understand anything of what had been said. Trofimov understood everything, but was unable to sympathize with the director. To be able to sympathize with somebody, one must immerse oneself in his state. But Trofimov was on Silvana's hook, like a fish, and felt only his own state.

Silvana and the businessman returned to the table and sat down. Silvana kept on staring at Vitali as though his forehead were covered with Arabic writing which was to be deciphered.

"Why is she staring?" Vitali was surprised.

"Ask her yourself."

Trofimov had mustered all his determination, as though for a parachute jump, and invited Silvana for a dance.

Silvana rose and followed Trofimov. A heterogeneous mass swayed near the orchestra. The dance was a slow one. Trofimov put his arm round Silvana's waist. It felt hard, as though it were in a plaster cast. Must be a corset, Trofimov thought. Silvana's breasts, pressed against him, were also hard, as though they were plastic. Their faces were at the same level. She isn't so tall after all, Trofimov realized. Not more than five foot eight.

There was not a single wrinkle under Silvana's eyes. The skin was as tight as on a drum.

It's not natural, Trofimov thought. She couldn't live all her life without laughing and weeping at all.

Nothing came from Silvana: neither warmth nor cold, and it suddenly seemed to Trofimov that he was dancing with a large doll with a hole in its back for a key to wind it up.

The dance ended. They returned to the table.

"Do you remember your film *All about Her?*" Trofimov asked Silvana.

"I've never heard of such a film," she replied.

"But..." Trofimov was perplexed. "It was on here...a long time ago."

Silvana's face assumed a slightly puzzled expression.

"What's she saying?" asked Vitali. The conversation had been in Italian.

"She said she didn't know the film *All about Her.*"

"Perhaps it isn't her at all," Vitali suggested.

Trofimov was puzzled. He saw that this Silvana and the other one were one and the same woman. But the Silvana of his dream was genuine, whereas this Silvana was artificial, like a stuffed form of the former Silvana.

"Perhaps that film was showing under a different title there," the businessman suggested. "Sometimes your film distributors invent new titles, more promising box-office-wise, as they think."

"Very strange," Trofimov mumbled.

He said it to himself rather than to the people round him. But it related not to the film distributors who invented new titles, but to the way his dream had realized. How his abstraction had materialized.

Had the *staphilococcus aureus* emerged and asked, "Well, how is it?" as was its habit, Trofimov would have felt better. He would have plunged into his usual emptiness and would have bided his time there. But even the *staphilococcus* was silent and did not raise its head. Could it have died? Silvana had introduced it thirty years before, and it was also she who destroyed it thirty years later.

Silvana invited Vitali to dance and got up. Vitali remained seated.

"You've invited to dance." Trofimov translated.

"I can't dance." Vitali was frightened.

"Get out of it yourself," Trofimov said.

Suddenly he felt calm. He had grown tired of the terrifying strain of a hooked fish. He wanted to sit more comfortably, relax, look and listen. Perhaps, not to look and listen, but to get up and go away, for example. Whichever suited him best.

For the first—and probably last—time in his life Vitali danced with an Italian film star in the press bar. He was a head shorter than her and saw before him only the jewelry displayed on her bosom like in the window of a jeweler's shop. Two large hands rested on his shoulders, and it seemed to him that two flat-irons were placed on them: they were so heavy and hot! From Silvana came emanations which made him shiver. Vitali felt as though he were in the transformer shed near their house maintenance service office, on which was painted a skull and cross-bones. He held on to Silvana but was somewhat apprehensive for his life. His life was not so important, but it was the only one he had.

Silvana bent and said something into his ear.

"Can't hear a damned thing!" Vitali shouted to her.

The Italian stared like a deaf-mute, trying to infer the meaning from the lip movements.

Vitali pointed to the orchestra, then to his ears, then made negative gestures before his face. All these signs were intended to show that he could not hear a damn thing.

Silvana nodded—so she had understood him—and pointed to the door. Vitali guessed: she was inviting him to go out and talk in the quiet of the fresh air.

"O.K.," he agreed. He offered Silvana his arm and they went out.

They made their way past the tables and past Terofimov and the businessman. The film director had vanished somewhere; he must have gone home to bed. Bow had "parked" at another table beside the Thumbelina-like blonde. He saw Vitali and Silvana and, forgetting the blonde, followed them with his eyes. He wanted to shout something to them, but was not quick enough.

"To hell with them," he decided.

"With whom?" asked Thumbelina.

"With all of them. They just put on airs."

Thumbelina's snub nose went up. Bow had sent everyone to hell except her. So she was superior to everyone. She was better than them all. However, something tormented Bow; one had crossed an ocean in a boat; another was a *grande professore;* the third, a foreigner. Everyone put his trump cards on the table. But Bow could only produce his roubles, which was something, but which was not enough.

"Don't think of them," Thumbelina said, sensing his mood, but not understanding the reason. "You're young and they're old."

Bow's spirits rose. How could he have overlooked such trump cards as youth and the prospect of a long life? He did not yet know that days lasted long, while decades flew by in a jiffy. In a moment or two he would no longer be young and would have to look for other trumps.

Silvana walked round the Moskva Hotel and entered it by the front door, sweeping past an imposing commissionaire, who looked like the president of a small republic. Vitali felt shy under his all-seeing, yet at the same time, vacant gaze. But when Silvana turned round, as if making sure that her companion was safe and sound, Vitali bravely walked after her although he had no idea as to where he was being led.

They entered a spacious lift, and already there it became clear to him that a different life was beginning. Vitali was being elevated to a new life.

The ceiling in Silvana's room was high, some eighteen feet. Another floor could be built in it, and a two-story flat would result with ceilings nine feet high, like flats in modern best-quality high rises.

"Very high," Vitali said, raising his hand.

Silvana looked up, but did not see anything of interest. She was used to ceilings as high as the one above her. Evidently the ceilings in her house were as high or, perhaps, even higher. She did not understand what had struck the Russian Bombard so.

"*Che?*" she said.

"Nothing. It's O.K.," said Vitali and dropped into a chair, suffering from a suffocating smell: in spite of its spaciousness, Silvana's room reeked of her perfume.

The mosquitoes will die off, Vitali thought. This was the only comforting aspect of it. The summer in Moscow was hot—just the right season for mosquitoes. And the mosquitoes had become fierce and had spread to the city. They bred even on asphalt. Now even clothes moths were unusual: they had learned to devour synthetic materials. But, on the other hand, what else could they eat if woolen thread was no longer made? It was either pure synthetic or half synthetic. People were also taught gradually to get accustomed to eating synthetic things. They said that synthetic black caviar had been manufactured. In appearance it did not differ from real caviar.

But what do moths and mosquitoes have to do with the story? Silvana stretched both arms towards Vitali and said something in her language. The words rapidly followed one another and sounded round and smooth like billiard balls. Vitali could not grasp the meaning, but guessed that the Italian was saying something very important to her. There were even tears in her eyes. She was dressed in clean clothes and her face was smooth from good food. Probably she ate real caviar by the spoonful.

"You've lived the life of Reilley," Vitali said to her. "If you lived as my Nadya does, you'd learn...Just look...the ceiling, the beads..."

"*Che?*" Silvana asked.

"Nothing. It's O.K. I said you didn't know what to do with yourself. People must overcome hardships. You can't live without hardships. It'd be corruption. Got it?"

Silvana started talking still more rapidly, her words poured out, collided and flew off in all directions. There were black rings under her eyes, like those which clowns have. Vitali was sorry for her.

"Don't!" he said. "Have you any grandchildren? You've lived in clover and in your old age you'll look after your grandchildren. And so you'll while away your time. What is life? Whiling away your time. If you are happy, time flies by quickly. And if you're bored, it drags on. For example, my relief is Kuzyayev. Yesterday I went to Flat 93 and agreed to connect their washing machine directly to the main. For twenty-five roubles. Twelve roubles fifty copecks for each of us. It was I who had arranged it, but he took Nikolai with him. And left me out of it. Was that honest? Eh? It wasn't. But I didn't say anything. I'm above that. You see? And you're saying..."

Silvana listened to Vitali attentively and trustfully, like a young girl. It seemed to her that he was saying something very important, was solving all her problems. She felt reassured by his voice and the confidence with which he was uttering the words of his strange language.

Each of them talked about his or her own problems, but it seemed to Silvana that this man understood her better than anyone else had ever done, and that she could confide in him to the end. She could confess something which she had been hiding even from herself.

"I'm fifty," she said. "But I haven't played my part yet. I haven't found my man yet. I have nothing, everything lies ahead, just as when I was twenty. But I'm fifty."

The Russian said something. She thought he had said: "One's flesh wears out more quickly than one's heart. The heart doesn't get old. It's always twenty. It's so with everybody and it's so with you."

"But I'm sorry for myself all the same. All my life I've been looking for Love, but I haven't found it."

"It's your fault."

"I know it's my fault. I'm guilty of compromise. I've been able to be satisfied with Not Him. I've been a coward. I've been afraid of remaining alone. I waited for Him while staying with someone else. But things do not work out that way. One must be able to take risks. You, for example, have risked your life—and you have won."

"Do you think so?"

"Of course. You're genuine. All the people I knew before trembled for their precious skin first and foremost. But you risked it. All the people I knew took care of their appearance and decorated themselves. But you—you don't dress up and do not follow the fashion. You even don't clean your nails. You can afford it because you're genuine. How ridiculous all these people in neckties and with handkerchiefs and wallets are beside you."

"Are you in love with me, or what?"

"No. I feel you are my equal. I am also genuine. And I am lonely."

Again tears welled up in Silvana's eyes.

"Well, don't." The Russian touched her hand lightly.

"I feel sad. I can't find peace. It's as though a great, real Love waited for me all my life and I failed to meet it. I played in films in order to become famous, broaden the circle of my acquaintances, and find Him. But neither beauty nor popularity—nothing can help. I know I am talented. I feel it, but a woman's main talent is to find Him with whom she can travel through life and be proud. But my time is slipping by."

"It's the same with everyone," the Russian said impassively.

"But I feel myself to be unique."

"Everyone thinks himself to be unique."

"What will you suggest?"

"Submit."

"I can't. I feel more acutely than before that I have a future. It seems to me that everything is still ahead and is yet to happen."

"It's old age. To young people everything seems to be behind. But to old people everything seems to be still ahead."

"You're cruel to people."

"I'm cruel to myself, too. One must be able to face the truth."

"Talented people are never old. Talent is a reflection of childhood."

"You may keep reassuring yourself as long as you want. But if you want my advice, here it is: conform to your season."

Silvana frowned.

"What do you mean?"

"Be like a tree. Like a river."

"But trees shed their leaves. And rivers freeze."

"So, shed your leaves and freeze! And don't be afraid. The main thing is dignity. People without dignity are ridiculous. Don't humiliate yourself. Don't lift your face to the back of your head. One must grow old with dignity."

Silvana stared at this Russian, her large eyes wide open. His expression was a little fatuous, and this fatuity reassured her somehow, for it seemed to be saying: what can you do? Man is part of nature and must obey its laws. As everybody and everything, except stones.

"But freezing and the shedding of leaves occur in the winter. And I'm still in the autumn."

"Get ready for the winter. Little by little."

"What about you?"

"Me, too."

They were marching in one and the same column. This long column was slowly moving into the winter. And beyond...

Silvana suddenly felt reassured, and this certainty calmed her down, and put everything in its place. Her confusion subsided. She became light-hearted. Even this morning she wondered why she had come here. Now she understood: it was worth her while traveling so far in order to find out that there would be nothing. Except winter. And it turned out to be good. She could calm down, look round and appreciate what there was. What there had been. Without constantly running somewhere, hurrying at a speed when all objects and people merged together into one continuous line. She could stop and look round: there were houses, there were people, and there was herself.

A water tap made a rumbling noise. Vitali immediately spotted the trouble by ear. He got up and went into the bathroom. He removed the cistern top and made the necessary adjustments.

Silvana followed him into the bathroom and stood there, watching.

"What is it?" Vitali asked.

"You are a man with whom I would not be afraid anywhere. Neither on sea, nor on land," said Silvana in Italian.

"I won't take anything," Vitali refused. "You're a guest, you know..."

It was still quite early. The commissionaire had not yet been relieved and looked fairly fresh, which meant that he had had his sleep out in his cubby hole.

"Good-bye, Sir," he said to Vitali.

Vitali did not reply. The commissionaire was far from his thoughts. In his mind's eye he saw the Italian's face, or rather her various faces. Her moods changed every moment, like a baby's: one moment she cried, and the next smiled. His Nadya was also like that. In general women were the same, be they Italian or Russian, millionairesses or paupers. They all wanted the same thing: to love and be loved. There was a saying: Love is blind. But this saying was very approximate. Of course, you could fall in love even with a hag, but such love would not last. Some time later you would understand that the object of your love was a hag.

That Italian mistook him for someone else. For the Frenchman who had crossed an ocean. And he—Vitali—had not denied it. So he had lied. Again he had lied. All the time he did nothing but lie and tell fibs. When it was necessary and when it wasn't necessary. Just out of habit. That Frenchman had drunk salt water, eaten raw fish and sailed among sharks for people's sakes, whereas he—Vitali—would not do a thing over and above his quota for anyone, even if all the pipes should burst and people in the entire neighborhood unit should have to walk in water knee deep.

Vitali did not notice how he had reached the Yauza River. On its bank St. Andronicus Monastery showed white and a lorry tire under its wall looked like a black spot.

Vitali rolled the tire into the water and without realizing it sat down on it and sailed down the river, using his hands like paddles. He was taken off in Norway.

Trofimov was returning from the bar in the small hours. He was walking through the city at night and heard his own footsteps. The houses he was passing by embodied the past and present and for the first time he realized how beautiful his city was. Previously he simply did not pay attention to it.

In general he did not pay attention to many things, as though he had lived seeing with only one eye and breathing with only one lung. And this early morning he breathed with his whole chest and saw with both eyes. And it proved to be twice as good as before.

Silvana had not returned and the plumber had disappeared somewhere. But it was all right. He was not a baby. He would find his bearings. As for Silvana, he had purged himself of her, and now he could take in more things: more of the city, more air, and more meaning.

"Thou shalt not make unto thee any graven image." This commandment ranked among "thou shalt not kill" and "thou shalt not steal." So making a graven image was the same as killing a living being. Killing part of oneself and placing a graven image in the vacant place. There would remain half of oneself and half of someone else. And exactly one half of oneself would be stolen.

Trofimov walked along Arbat Street. All of Trofimov. There was no one else and nothing else in him: neither Silvana, nor the staphilococcus, nor any gnawing dissatisfaction, nor any covetous desire of a different, unattainable life. He felt like that old, fifteen-year-old boy. His whole life was ahead and he could start winning it again and conquering it like a mountain climber, but not from the foot of the mountain, but from the already conquered heights, climbing still higher and along a steeper slope. To the very top. In order to be able to stand up, look round, and hoist his flag.

Trofimov had not spent himself over the past thirty years. He seemed to have stayed in a refrigerator and had now stepped out, swaying, into the summer, feeling a powerful reserve of life and trust in the world.

His wife and son were asleep, each in his little burrow and even in their sleep felt secure: no one would come and devour them, because they were guarded by their master. Trofimov felt a surge of tenderness and gratitude for the fact that they existed. For being allowed to defend two beings: a woman and a boy. They were his woman and his boy. They needed him. So he was not alone.

As usual there was no bread. Only the same moldy hunks covered with ants. The ants scurried about, tiny and graceful like dashes and hyphens on a typewritten page. It was strange that these creatures were called by the ominous word "termites" and could devour a wooden house, for example.

His wife appeared in the doorway suddenly and noiselessly, like a vision.

"Do you want me to go and buy bread?" Trofimov suggested.

"I can go myself."

"Let's go together."

"Why?"His wife did not understand.

"Together," Trofimov repeated, as though explaining the meaning of the word together.

She stared at his face shyly, like a girl—the same girl who had thrown herself under his feet on the skating rink. She stood in the doorway, holding onto the door post and not daring to go in, as though it were not her house.

"Come in," Trofimov invited her. "Why are you standing there?"

Born in Leningrad, Victoria Tokareva graduated from the Script Writers Department of the Moscow Institute of Cinematography in 1967. She has written a number of successful books of short stories and several film scripts. The film script Mimino, *which she co-authored with Georgi Gabriadze, was awarded the Gold Prize* at the Tenth International Moscow Film Festival. The author now lives in Moscow. This story was translated by Vladimir Korotky.

For readers who can't read...

Greek, Arabic, Chinese, Japanese, Dutch, Norwegian, Chukchi, Finnish, Hindi, Turkish, Urdu, Hebrew, Russian, Vietnamese, Portuguese, etc., etc.

Short Story International takes you to all points of the compass, to anywhere in the world. There are intriguing stories waiting for you in future issues of SSI—stories that will involve you in corners of this world you've never seen...and in worlds outside this one...with glimpses into the future as well as the past, revealing fascinating, universal truths that bypass differences in language and point up similarities in people.

Send in the coupon below and every other month SSI will take you on a world cruise via the best short stories being published throughout the world today—the best entertainment gleaned from the work of the great creative writers who are enhancing the oldest expression of the entertainment arts—the short story.

A Harvest of the World's
Best Contemporary Writing Selected
and Published Every Other Month

Please enter my subscription to
Short Story International
P.O. Box 405, Great Neck, New York 11022
Six Issues for $24, U.S. & U.S. Possessions
Canada $27 (US), All Other Countries $29 (US)
Enclosed is my check for $ _____ for _____ subscriptions.

Name _____

Address _____

City _____ State _____ Zip _____

Country _____

Please check   ☐ *New Subscription*   ☐ *Renewal*

Gift for:

Name _____

Address _____

City _____ State _____ Zip _____

Country _____

Please check ▢ New Subscription   ▢ Renewal

Gift for:

Name _____

Address _____

City _____ State _____ Zip _____

Country _____

Please check ▢ New Subscription   ▢ Renewal

Gift for:

Name _____

Address _____

City _____ State _____ Zip _____

Country _____

Please check ▢ New Subscription   ▢ Renewal

Gift for:

Name _____

Address _____

City _____ State _____ Zip _____

Country _____

Please check ▢ New Subscription   ▢ Renewal

Gift for:

Name _____

Address _____

City _____ State _____ Zip _____

Country _____

Please check ▢ New Subscription   ▢ Renewal

Gift for:

Name _____

Address _____

City _____ State _____ Zip _____

Country _____

Please check ▢ New Subscription   ▢ Renewal

For the young people in your life...

The world of the short story for young people is inviting, exciting, rich in culture and tradition of near and far corners of the earth. *You* hold the key to this world...a world you can unlock for the young in your life...and inspire in them a genuine love for reading. We can think of few things which will give them as much lifelong pleasure as the habit of reading.

Seedling Series is directed to elementary readers (grades 4-7), and **Student Series** is geared to junior and senior high school readers.

Our stories from all lands are carefully selected to promote and strengthen the reading habit.

Give a Harvest of the World's Best Short Stories
Published Four Times a Year for Growing Minds.

Please enter my subscription(s) to:

_____ **Seedling Series: Short Story International**
$16 U.S. & U.S. Possessions
Canada $18 (U.S.) All Other Countries $19 (U.S.)

_____ Student Series: Short Story International
$18 U.S. & U.S. Possessions
Canada $20 (U.S.) All Other Countries $21 (U.S.)

Mail with check to:
Short Story International
P.O. Box 405, Great Neck, New York 11022
Donor: Name _____
Address _____
City _____ State _____ Zip _____
Country _____

Send To: Name _____
Address _____
City _____ State _____ Zip _____
Country _____
Please check ☐ *New Subscription* ☐ *Renewal*

Send To: Name _____
Address _____
City _____ State _____ Zip _____
Country _____
Please check ☐ *New Subscription* ☐ *Renewal*